Look what people are saying about Jule McBride...

"Great details, a wonderfully sexy hero, hot sex and an intriguing plot."
—*Romantic Times BOOKreviews* on *The Pleasure Chest*

"*Night Pleasures* lives up to its title."
—*The Best Reviews*

"A fun read."
—*Romantic Times BOOKreviews* on *Cold Case, Hot Bodies*

"An exciting political romance."
—*The Best Reviews* on *Naughty by Nature*

"Romance, mystery and interesting, attractive characters, all brewed into a delicious concoction."
—*Romantic Times BOOKreviews* on *Something in the Water...*
(A 4½ star Top Pick!)

Books by Jule McBride

HARLEQUIN BLAZE

Jule McBride

NAKED ATTRACTION

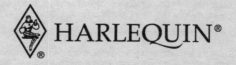

TORONTO • NEW YORK • LONDON
AMSTERDAM • PARIS • SYDNEY • HAMBURG
STOCKHOLM • ATHENS • TOKYO • MILAN • MADRID
PRAGUE • WARSAW • BUDAPEST • AUCKLAND

Recycling programs
for this product may
not exist in your area.

ISBN-13: 978-0-373-79464-5
ISBN-10:   0-373-79464-9

NAKED ATTRACTION

www.eHarlequin.com

Printed in U.S.A.

ABOUT THE AUTHOR

A native West Virginian, Jule McBride had her dream to write romances come true in the nineties with the publication of her debut novel, *Wild Card Wedding*. It received a *Romantic Times BOOKreviews* Reviewer's Choice Award for Best First Series Romance. Since then, the author has been nominated for multiple awards, including two lifetime achievement awards. She has written for several series, and currently makes her happy home at Harlequin Blaze. A prolific writer, she has almost fifty titles to her credit.

1

WHEN ELLIE LEE STRETCHED and opened her eyes, she found herself staring straight into Robby Robriquet's baby blues. They captivated her gaze, warmed her insides, then continued holding her attention as surely as his arms had held her the previous night. "How long have you been watching me?" she croaked sleepily.

"All my life."

"Impossible. You were born first."

"All your life," he corrected.

Shifting her gaze, she let it drift down a hard, muscular bare chest coated with wild, tangled raven hair. She eyed the sheet wound around his torso, then returned her attention to his face, her lips parting in frank appreciation of his heart-stopping good looks.

Damn, she thought. They just didn't make many studs like Robby, especially not around Banner, Mississippi. He had a strong, Romanesque nose, unusually full lips, a face so sculpted that it could have been crafted from marble. His eyes were as piercing as the rays of a hot sun, as blue as a summer sky, and as deep as an ocean.

She had blue eyes, also, and dark hair, just as he, and if the truth be told, she'd started dreaming years ago about how cute their babies would look. She'd had a crush on Robby since she'd first laid eyes on him, when she was twelve years old, but only in the past year, since he'd finished his M.B.A. and returned to Banner, had he finally realized she'd turned into a woman.

So much for all the heartbreak years ago. Countless times, she'd put on sexy hot pants and halter tops, hoping to wow him if he came to the Lees' house to visit her middle brother, Cordy, often with J. D. Johnson in tow. Ellie's best friend, Susannah, had been just as lovesick, but J.D. had been her focus. The two girls had tried everything to get the boys' attention, whether getting stuck while climbing trees, or shrieking like banshees while practicing gymnastics in the yard.

Nothing had seemed to work. The boys would run off, to hunt or fish, totally oblivious. Everything was different now, though. J.D. and Susannah had been married for six years. And exactly six months ago, Robby had dragged Ellie to bed, acting as proprietary as a caveman. Ever since, they'd managed to meet at every possible moment, despite hectic schedules.

That was the other great thing about Robby, she thought, still eyeing him. He worked even harder than she, a trait she'd never found in another man. In fact, she thought Robby worked too hard, something she'd previously never guessed she could see as a flaw in another human being. But how could she help it? Business was important, but she wanted Robby in bed all the time, too, and because he always said he had to work, it could be downright maddening.

Yes, now she understood all the young men she'd discarded during her own college years. Often they'd complain, calling her a workaholic, but now….

Robby was gazing at her bare breasts, his dazed eyes darkening with lust. "Hey, gorgeous," she whispered. "I think I'm reading your mind."

"What? Like Mama Ambrosia?"

Mama Ambrosia was a local fortune-teller. Ellie shook her

head. Lifting her hands, she squeezed his shoulders, drawing him closer, enjoying the warmth and smoothness of his skin. "No. What I see in your thoughts is far too suggestive for a stranger's clairvoyant eyes, even a professional's."

He glanced at the clock, his glistening teeth flashing as he smiled. "Well, sweetheart," he drawled, "I figure we've got time for a quickie before we get to work and have to pretend we're only colleagues."

"You've been a bad boy on the job," she returned, stroking his pectorals with a fingernail.

He was all innocence. "Bad?"

"A hand up my skirt during a meeting. Pinching my butt at the water cooler. A box of condoms appearing magically in my purse," she enumerated.

"That wasn't me," he defended. "That was the condom fairy." She smiled. "If we don't tell my father about our affair soon," she said, dragging his mouth down for a quick, wet kiss, "he's going to guess." Her father, otherwise known as Daddy Eddie, was the owner of Lee Polls, a century-old family-run polling company for which both she and Robby worked.

"Then we'd better hurry and have sex, so you'll have time to run home, change and do something about your mussed hair."

She smirked. "You really are a workaholic. It's Saturday."

"And I've got to work, anyway."

Frowning, she considered. She loved Robby, she really did, but she was beginning to wonder if he'd ever feel completely comfortable in his own skin. He'd been so young when he'd lost his mother, only three, and he scarcely remembered her. Worse, his dad, Charlie, had seemed to go off the deep end after the loss, taking up drinking and gambling. At least, that was the story around town.

He'd been in prison for years now, for manslaughter. Even before that, Charlie had embarrassed his son. Nightly, he could be found spending his paycheck at a local watering hole called the Night Rider, running up a tab, then going further into debt by placing bets with a man suspected of being the town bookie, Max Sweeney. Sheriff Kemp had often looked the other way, just to spare Robby, who, from an early age, had so often dragged his dad out of the bar and home for the night.

Manslaughter had been too much to overlook, though. And while Ellie was glad her own father, Daddy Eddie, had intervened and offered Robby a job at Lee Polls after high school, her heart had broken when she'd seen just how hard Robby had worked, losing too much sleep, not to mention nights and weekends, always sweating the smallest details.

His determination had earned Daddy Eddie's trust, and he'd often claimed Robby was more valuable than all his own sons combined. Not that Ellie's ne'er-do-well brothers had minded, not even when Daddy Eddie had sent Robby to college and graduate school. Robby had worked odd jobs, too, not wanting to take charity and trying to make clear he was pulling himself up by the bootstraps. Now, no matter how successful he became, Robby seemed to think he owed Daddy Eddie something, which he didn't.

Yes, that was the problem. Robby idolized her dad, since Daddy Eddie was the exact opposite of what Robby's had been, but it was sure putting a damper on romance. Robby feared Daddy Eddie's reaction—despite all that he'd achieved, was he good enough for the man's only daughter?

Robby had turned out to be loyal and hardworking, whereas every one of Daddy Eddie's sons—Gil, Cordy and Kyle—was worthless when it came to running Lee Polls. They preferred to hunt, fish, play golf and chase women. So, although it was a family business, Ellie and Robby, who reported directly to Daddy Eddie, did most of the work.

"You're really going into the office?" she asked.

"You're not?"

"Only after I meet Susannah for breakfast." Saturday breakfast was usually set aside for her best friend.

Robby's voice was low, sexy. "Then we'd better get a move on. Kiss me, baby."

She wiggled her eyebrows as he pushed a lock of hair away from her eyes. "Where?"

"Here." Leaning, he gingerly toyed with her breast, brushing the gold charm that hung from a chain around her neck. Engraved on the metal were the words *Remember the Time.* She and Susannah had the matching necklaces made years ago, and both still wore them always.

Robby palmed a breast, bending and roughening the sensitive skin with his chin stubble before flicking a tongue across the nipple, sending a shock of longing to her core. Her hips arched, her chin tilted back and for a moment, she simply got lost in the pleasure. Easy enough, as both hands found her, pushing her breasts upward from beneath. As he squeezed hard, her mind spun dizzily, her nipples tightening further, straining for the touch.

Throatily, she whispered, "I thought I was supposed to kiss you, not the other way around."

He merely locked his lip to a bud and kept suckling, the silken wetness making her shiver. With a sigh, she pressed her thighs together tightly, as if to hold in the delicious sensations he was soliciting. Soon, he'd be on top of her, she knew. Or she'd be on top of him. And then...

He blew on the flesh he'd just dampened, then caught a nipple and rolled it between his fingers, causing goose bumps of anticipation to rise all over her skin. "Oh, Robby..."

"Hmm?"

"Nothing." But she wanted to say she could come from nothing more than this kind of sweet teasing. She gasped as his huge, warm hand slid downward, over her ribs, then her belly. Arrowing his fingertips, he urged apart her smooth thighs as his mouth found her neck. He was all tongue now—stroking the column beneath her chin as she shifted her weight and let him untangle her legs.

"Wider," he drawled softly.

Was this really happening? she wondered vaguely as she gave him increased access. Was she really sharing a bed with the heartthrob of her adolescent years? It had become clear the relationship was headed for so much more. Already, they were in serious terrain. Inseparable and intense, their lives completely intertwined.

A soft senseless murmur escaped her lips as his fingers grasped her curls, toying with them. He tugged playfully, then a slick finger slid open her lower lips completely, and she could only suck another breath through clenched teeth as he circled the nub of her clitoris. "You're so good…" she whispered. "But it could be better…"

"Better?"

His voice was catching now, and the one word was nearly lost in his throat, since his breath was quickening. Yes, she thought hazily, as he probed where she was growing so slick and damp for him. As he thrust a finger inside, testing the moist heat, preparing her, she arched once more, turning in his arms, her nipples peaking, becoming painfully taut, every fiber of her being craving his mouth once more.

Instinctively, her hand rose, threading in his hair, her heart stuttering as the wild, bed-tossed strands of jet-black ran through her fingers feeling like water. As he pushed another finger inside her, she gasped, her fist tightening, closing around the wisps of his hair, pulling his face closer so her mouth could brush his. Electrifying, she thought. Heavenly.

Then for another moment, she shut her eyes. Sensations

cascaded over her like a waterfall. Tension built, climbing, threatening to shatter. When she opened her eyes again, he was watching her, his blue eyes as warm as summer, his smile inviting. "Feels good, huh?"

His hairy chest slowly rising and falling with the pace of his increasing breath. "Yeah," she whispered as he visibly shuddered, then slid a finger from inside her and moved on top of her.

She loved him. That's all she could think as she looked into his eyes, her heart racing. But she had to get him to commit. She'd wanted him her whole life, and this past six months had been pure torture. Always, he'd been the only man for her. Sure, she'd fooled around at college, but no one could hold a candle to Robby. She wanted more….

"Honey," she began, her voice a soft drawl, her heart hammering harder as his legs fell between hers. She could feel the heat and power of his erection now, touching her through the sheet that had tangled between them.

He rested on an elbow, a hand beneath his cheek and flashed a bad-boy grin. "Yes, honey?"

"I want to ask you something."

"Anything."

"When are we going to tell my dad?"

"Tell him?"

"You know. About us."

They were at a crossroads. Daddy Eddie was retiring in just one more week, and he'd already told her he was naming her head of the company. President, she thought now, with a sigh of happiness. It was more than she'd dreamed possible. Robby aside, running Lee Polls had always been her dream, too. The venerable company had been housed in Banner since 1898, and a Lee had always been at the helm. Never a woman, of course.

Until now. That was mostly due to the fact that none of

Ellie's brothers had possessed an interest in facts and figures, nor the knack for math that it took to analyze statistics. By contrast, Ellie could eat and breathe mathematics. And so, it had been she, not her male siblings, who had spent hours visiting her dad at work.

By age five, she'd picked out her own office, right next door to Daddy Eddie, and on her tenth birthday, he'd placed a gold plaque on the door, engraved with her name.

"How 'bout that, Ellie girl," her dad had said. "One day, all this really will be yours."

Now that same office was stacked high with statistical manuals and files of client information. Soon, as her father had always promised, that old plaque would come down and the new one would replace it. The one that said, "President."

"Daddy's retiring in a week," she suddenly whispered in a rush. "We don't have much time, Robby. I want him to know…how things are between us."

Dammit, why was she so spineless? So closemouthed? Why couldn't she just say she really wanted to get married? After all, her best friend, Susannah, had been married for six years now, even if her and J.D.'s road had turned a little rocky. And yet…even though she was a modern woman it wasn't really a woman's place to ask a man for his hand. Hell, she was going to be the president of a company by this time next week, but there were still some things in life a man had to do.

Besides, there was another uncomfortable fact, in that Robby was going to report to her. As macho as he was, she could only hope he wouldn't have trouble dealing with that. Certainly, they'd traded a lot of jokes about the possibility. And he didn't seem to mind…

Why should he? she thought now. The company had been in her family for a century, and she'd grown up under the strict tutelage of her father. Oh, Robby was good, of course. Better than she at some aspects of the job, in fact. Maybe he was even completely on a par. But the bottom line remained. Having a Lee in the top spot was an unbroken tradition. "Really," she began again. "We need to talk to Daddy." She started to continue, but something in his eyes stopped her, and instead, she squinted and said, "What?"

"I…I have something to ask you."

Her heart pounded against her ribs. He was going to ask her to marry him, she realized. Right now. In this very instant of time. Inadvertently, her lips parted and she breathed in deeply, bracing herself. She wanted to savor this moment, so she could remember it always. "Yes?"

"Would you mind terribly if…"

Her cheeks heated, her heart bursting with feeling. He was such a guy. A man's man. Of course it wasn't easy for him to ask… "If?" she encouraged.

"If your dad gave me the job?" He paused. "You know, running the company."

Everything froze. For a second, all thoughts were vanquished from her mind. Surely, she hadn't heard right. "What?"

"He…pulled me aside last week."

"Last week!" That was impossible. Daddy Eddie had pulled her aside last week.

"I know you're going to be mad, but just hear me out. I think he knows, or suspects, or…"

"Suspects what?"

"That we…"

Barely aware of her actions, and working on sheer revulsion, she squirmed out from under him and got up, taking the sheet with her. "That we were sleeping together?" she managed, whirling to face him. Not that she knew why, but just now, he'd become a stranger before her very eyes.

"I think it's possible," Robby said, reaching and trying to

grab her hand, which she snatched away. "Oh, c'mon, don't be a spoilsport," he teased.

"Spoilsport?" she could only echo, turning on him, then leaning to gather her clothes. Quickly, she slipped a knit dress over her head and shoved her feet into ballet flats, not bothering to find her panties as he rose from the bed and closed the distance between them.

Two large hands clamped on her waist, and against her will, she shuddered as he drew her against him. She might hate him at the moment, but his body was hard, hot, male and naked, and he'd left her half aroused. Suddenly, she ached for him.

"Your dad and I talked about it," he said firmly.

Didn't he understand that he might as well have slapped her in the face? That this was the ultimate in the loss of trust? "Whatever we've done here…" she managed to begin, her voice raspy, altered by the horrible sting of betrayal. "In this bedroom, and at my house…"

"I didn't tell him anything, Ellie."

"That's not the point."

"And the point is?"

"Look, we never talked about it. But mixing business and pleasure was a really bad idea. I see that now," she managed.

His grip tightened. "Liar. You know how serious this is," he muttered, sounding stunned.

"Well," she defended. "I guess I did feel we had an understanding…that you and I were a couple."

"We are."

"But we were going to tell Daddy about us. You and me, Robby. Together."

Dammit, this was par for the course. Like when her dad and brothers created their own little club. Her mom had tried to turn her into a girly girl, but Ellie had inherited her father's talent and knack for business. And now…she was nowhere.

Left out in the cold. If the job was really Robby's...she could never look at him again.

Her words were barely audible. "How could you?"

He knew what the family company meant. It was in her blood and belonged to her.

"You think I sabotaged you?"

"Did you?"

He was starting to look furious. "He came to me, Ellie, not the other way around." Despite the fire in his blue eyes, which were turning to ice, an uncharacteristic pleading tone had crept into his voice. Not that she cared. He was the one who'd put himself between a rock and a hard place.

He added, "What should I do, Ellie?"

"Take the job, I guess," she burst out. So what if Daddy Eddie was her father, not his? So what if she'd worked around the clock for years, just as Robby had? Once more, her lips parted in astonishment. Suddenly, she blurted out, "I don't believe you—"

He was incredulous. "You think I'm lying?"

"Yes. It just can't be true." Quickly, she wiggled from his grasp, strode to the bedside table and lifted the phone receiver.

She caught him squinting at her. "What are you doing, Ellie?"

"Calling Daddy Eddie."

Robby's face fell. "Don't."

"Why?" Her eyes pierced his as Daddy Eddie's phone rang. "I'm sure he wanted to tell you."

"Well, he didn't, now did he? And I think you're lying."

"Why would I?"

She offered a mean shrug. "Spite?"

Robby's gorgeous blue eyes widened a fraction. "Look, Ellie, I know you're upset, but we can work through this..."

Ellie didn't see how. Thankfully, her dad finally picked up. "Daddy?" Before he could respond, she continued. "I...uh, stopped by Robby Robriquet's place just now, to…uh, pick up some files for work—"

"This early in the morning?"

"Yes. And it's not that earl—"

"For a Satur—"

Damn her dad for interrupting and trying to distract her. "Daddy," she said in a rush. "Robby swears—"

"I didn't swear," interjected Robby. "I just said—"

"That you're promoting him over me next week when you retire, and he's been chosen to run Lee Polls." Been chosen. The words echoed in her mind. How could her own father deny her? "I told him this was ludicrous. Completely, utterly impossible. And I know you'll be glad that I stepped in and corrected him.

"Why, you and I have talked about my appointment for years, ever since I was a little girl. Right, Daddy? And you know I have the highest credentials, not to mention more time with the company, overall. I mean, if you count the years I worked there in high school…"

Realizing her dad hadn't jumped to her defense, she let her voice trail off. A long pause followed. And then her daddy said the impossible, "It's true, Ellie."

She barely heard what he said after that. Just a jumble of justifications, really. He suspected she was going to want to get married and have a family someday, he said, and that he didn't want work to get in her way forever, since he loved her so much. He'd always felt badly that her brothers hadn't done their share, so thank God for Robby. Besides which, her mother agreed Ellie needed to focus more on other aspects of life.

"Like marriage? Having a family?" Her jaw dropped. Sure, she'd been about to propose to Robby, but that was when she was going to be president of her company, too. But now…

"How far back in time did you have to go," she finally

managed, "to find a speech like that one, Daddy? The Middle Ages? The Dark Ages? Did you go to a museum?" How had her father, who had always been so supportive, morphed into a caveman? "Did Mom talk you into this?" she accused.

"No, Ellie, and this has nothing to do with your qualifications. You know that. When it came down to brass tacks, I just want a man running my ship. And that's my right."

"That's illegal, I think," she muttered.

"Well, I doubt my own daughter's going to take me to court."

"Don't count on it."

"You don't see it now," he said firmly. "But you're going to want more out of life down the road."

"I've been running your ship for years," she ground out, her eyes now fixing on Robby's. Seconds ago, those gorgeous baby blues had looked so sweet and nonthreatening. They'd turned her knees to water. Now they seemed cold and calculating, vicious and predatory. What had she ever seen in him?

"Yes…I've been helping you for years, Dad. My good-for-nothing brothers, your lousy sons made sure of that!"

"Ellie, please hear me out—"

She slammed down the phone, fuming. Lee Polls was hers. It was in her history and her blood. Nobody was taking it away, not even her lover—ex-lover, she mentally amended— Robby Robriquet.

Except he had.

She grabbed her purse and headed for the door and when he grasped her from behind, she shook off his touch. "Bastard," she muttered, hating that her body still tingled from his touch as she opened the door and stepped outside, into air that was crisp for November in Mississippi. "Get away from me."

"Ellie," he called from the porch as she headed for her car. "You didn't even let me talk. I want to be with you. Always. Forever. You and me. We can work this out."

"Yeah, right," she shouted. "You want to get married and have kids and—"

"Yes! Yes, that's exactly what I want!"

"And I'll cook and clean for you while you go off to my office."

"Dammit, Ellie!"

If it had been any other company but Lee Polls, maybe she could have gotten over it. Her heart stretched to breaking. "That company is mine! Mine!"

"Come back, Ellie!"

"No...you go back inside and put on some clothes, Robby," she called over her shoulder. "Otherwise Sheriff Kemp might arrest you for indecent exposure. And besides, don't you have to hurry up and put on your suit and tie? Don't you have a job to go to? My job? In the company that belongs to my family?"

"Dammit, I know this is sensitive."

"You're just like your father," she yelled, striking the lowest blow she could think of. "You wanted my job and you took it, but you're not getting me, too."

Maybe he said something else, but she'd never know. She was already in her car. Tears were flowing freely, and she didn't bother to stop them. By the time she'd become cognizant of her actions, she was sobbing deeply, her shoulders shaking. Through a haze of tears, she just kept moving. She stopped at her house and packed bags that would last her a while. At first, she had no idea where she might go.

Hodges Motor Lodge was an option, but that was too local. Besides, everyone would know to look for her there, since it was the only motel in town. So she made a plane reservation. Yes, she needed a vacation. Screw Lee Polls. Daddy Eddie and Robby had decided they could run the place without her, so let them.

"Just see how far they get!" she declared. They could never find the Thomas files, they didn't have a clue about how to land that lucrative account with the Clovis family, or the contracts for upcoming national elections. Besides, her own client list was on her laptop, which she would take with her, and they'd play hell trying to decipher her notes.

"Within a week, the whole place will shut down," she vowed. Once her bags were piled high in her car, she sped toward Delia's Diner. Thankfully, as soon as she had breakfast, and told her best friend, Susannah, about her plan, she'd be getting far away from Banner, Mississippi.

But Susannah wasn't at Delia's yet. So Ellie sat in the car sobbing some more, which felt good, then she finally shoved on her sunglasses to hide her eyes. Delia's Diner was gossip central.

She waved at a few people inside the restaurant, ordered coffee and noted that Sheriff Kemp was at the counter, flirting with Delia again. Ellie had to concentrate on not crying now; otherwise, everybody in Banner would know something was wrong and start grilling her. So she stared into space, barely noticing when her best friend came in and seated herself in the booth.

Susannah was the sister Ellie had never had. As much as Ellie loved her, though, she was always embroiled in some new drama surrounding her husband, J.D. Ever since he'd become a country star, the marriage had been heading south, and all the arguments about leaving the man had been discussed before today. So, even though Ellie was numb, her mind reeling from her own life-altering circumstances, Susannah didn't even notice, due to her own difficulties. This made it easy to order breakfast while murmuring all the usual consolations.

Even when Susannah announced she was finally leaving her husband, Ellie merely kept nodding. Susannah threatened this at least once a month, after all. Almost as often as she threatened to kill J.D.

The man was still breathing, however, and Ellie doubted

Susannah would ever free herself from the increasingly problematic relationship. Suddenly, Susannah pushed unruly wisps of blond hair from her eyes, and said, "You've been crying, Ellie."

Only then did Ellie notice she'd removed her sunglasses. She guessed she'd removed them when Delia had put down their breakfast plates. Eggs could be a little unappealing seen through dark lenses. "All morning," she said, although it wasn't strictly true.

"I'm sorry. I've been so fixated on J.D. What's wrong?"

The story came pouring out. When Ellie was finished, Susannah gasped. "And Robby accepted the job?"

Ellie nodded.

"That snake in the grass! What are you going to do?"

In that instant, Ellie knew. "Go to New York and start another polling business to compete with Daddy and Robby."

She'd been considering a vacation, but why not make it permanent? She'd done business in New York and had contacts there. Maybe such a plan would work. Had Susannah, herself, been sincere about her own plans to leave J.D.? "Come with me, Susannah."

"To New York?" Susannah said. "To do what?"

Ellie's mind was racing as she started offering ideas, then she finished by declaring, "To have sex with a lot of men. Every guy I can."

She could see Susannah's throat working as she swallowed hard. "That…uh, sounds ambitious."

Ellie almost smiled. "I've always been ambitious," she agreed.

"Well…okay. Yes. I'll come with you."

"Good." But could Ellie really make this work? Could she build a competitive polling company from the ground up, then maybe even use it to take over Lee Polls? More important, could she find a man sexy enough to replace Robby Robriquet?

2

Eleven Months Later

NEWSPAPER BUSINESS REPORTER Derrick Mills wasn't nearly as good-looking as Robby. He was taller, less stocky, with dark hair and eyes. Still, Ellie assured herself as she took in his tailored gray suit, she would have jumped into the sack with him, if not for one little problem. Derrick was married. So she'd just have to stay on topic and continue answering his questions. Most important, she needed to gauge when it would be best to drop her bombshell.

She'd been planning her strategy for months, and now the moment was near. She had to fight not to grin. Yes, the gimmick she was going to announce would kill a few birds with one stone. She'd generate business, create media buzz for herself and erase the memory of Robby Robriquet from her life forever. And why not? She believed in her skills of statistical analysis, didn't she? And she wanted to find someone she'd like as much as Robby.

Love as much. When the words entered her consciousness, she tried to ignore them. But she had loved the man. Surely, no one would ever turn her on in the same way. Besides, for so long, she'd just unconsciously assumed she and Robby would have…

A wedding.

A house with a picket fence in Banner, Mississippi.

Babies.

And, of course, share the joy of combined careers. Lastly, the sparks of their passion would never burn out. With one look, Robby had always set her on fire. In the office of Lee Polls, they'd shared so many laughs, too, especially since they hadn't been able to keep their hands off each other. Now, just thinking about her ex-lover, her skin warmed, her heart missed a beat, her palms started to sweat....

"Ms. Lee?"

She snapped to attention, then searched her mind, trying to remember what the interviewer had asked. "Was my decision to start Future Trends influenced by my father's appointment of Robby Robriquet to run Lee Polls?" she prompted.

"Yes," Derrick returned. "Was it?"

"Of course not!"

"You're sure?"

"Absolutely. I'm very happy here. Who wouldn't be?" She waved a hand to call his attention to the surroundings. She'd revamped a two-bedroom apartment in a brownstone, the same one she'd initially shared with Susannah when they'd first arrived in New York nearly a year ago.

Since then, Susannah had reunited with J.D. and Ellie had retooled the place into an office. New gray carpet, simple black lacquer desks and classic plum window treatments had made the apartment look trendy and upscale.

"But it was assumed you, not Robby Robriquet, would have that position?" Derrick Mills prompted.

Silently, she damned the reporter for rubbing salt in the old wound. "Not really," she denied. "Or, to whatever extent I assumed that, I'm not sorry." She offered a wry smile, hoping Derrick would fill in the blanks.

"Not sorry that Lee Polls has trended downward in sales

and contracts? Some of its oldest customers have jumped ship since you left, you know."

"Sometimes it's either sink or swim."

"And you're swimming while Lee Polls is sinking?"

"You said that, Mr. Mills, not I."

"But where do your ultimate loyalties lie?"

"With myself." She arched a brow. "I mean, do you think I should retain family loyalties merely because Lee Polls has been run by Lees for so long?"

"I wondered."

"None whatsoever. Business is business, Mr. Mills. We all know that."

"Clearly, you do. No wonder you're so successful. Many might have experienced the Robriquet appointment as a setback, but instead, you opened Future Trends within a week of your father's decision. There have even been rumors, saying that you now intend to sell your new business already, for a hefty profit, once more proving your lack of sentimentality."

"Quite the contrary. I'm looking for acquisitions, although not for sentimental reasons."

"Lee Polls?" He eyed her. "Are you considering buying your family's company and merging it with Future Trends?"

"Again, you said it, not I." She laughed lightly. "Although nothing's in the works quite yet." But if she was quoted in the newspaper, Robby might start to sweat, she thought. And after what he'd done to her, she wouldn't mind making him squirm.

"People might take such a move as vindictive."

"Well, I've never cared what people think of me."

"Fair enough."

"But as I said, I've got no feelers out right now." She smiled once more. "I'd need to find more office space first, anyway."

"Three rooms could be cramped after a merger," he conceded, glancing from where they were seated to what had been the living room a few months ago.

Following his gaze, Ellie tried not to grimace. Her only employee, Angelina Carrella, had seemed excellent on many levels, at least initially. She was neat, prompt and efficient. However, love had entered her life, and now the girl was ruined. An engagement had followed, and ever since, Angelina was distracted and absentminded. Yes, in only a few short months, she'd transformed from a demure assistant into a brazen spitfire who spent half the day on the phone with her fiancé, Antonio, or the various relatives from whom she was soliciting funds to pay for an absurdly lavish wedding.

Each day, Ellie was treated to the very last thing she needed to see—pictures of gowns, flowers, cakes and bridesmaids' gifts. One minute, the wedding would be black and white, then pink and blue, then red and green. Plans had begun for Valentine's day, then Christmas, then Antonio's birthday. Every step in the direction of finalizing a decision caused lengthy phone fights.

Even worse, despite Ellie's clear instructions to behave while Derrick Mills was on the premises, at least, Antonio had now arrived to take his sweetheart to lunch. By the looks of it, and the very loud smacking sounds, if the two didn't leave soon, they might well wind up making love on Angelina's desk.

Ignoring the trajectory of her interviewer's gaze, Ellie continued, "Well, most of the analytical work is done by computer here, and I often meet clients in their own offices."

Derrick Mills was still watching the couple. "Looks like you've got lovebirds around."

So much for ignoring them. "She was an excellent assistant before the engagement," Ellie quipped with a wry smile.

"A wedding can be so exciting," Derrick said on a sigh.

Great. He was a romantic. Ellie couldn't help but notice

he began toying with his wedding ring. "A newlywed yourself?" she guessed.

"Almost a year ago."

About the time Ellie was leaving Robby. "I'm happy for you," she managed, very much doubting she sounded sincere.

Not that he seemed to notice. When his eyes found hers again, they held that dopey dazed look of the truly loved. "No man in your life at the moment?" he prodded.

She tamped down the images the words conjured…Robby's hot body slick with soapsuds in the shower, asleep on his back with a sheet draped over his hips like a loincloth, lifting her off her feet and whirling her in a circle. "Afraid I have too little time."

His eyes were on Angelina and Antonio again, and when she followed his gaze once more, Ellie realized it was no wonder. The Latin lothario had his sweetie nearly backed against the desk now, his hands on her hips, a huge, lusty Cheshire grin on his face. The hem of Angelina's skirt was rising dangerously high on her thigh. Heat rose in Ellie's cheeks. The other day, she'd returned from a client meeting and found the couple nearly sprawled across the couch. Well, maybe that was an exaggeration, but there was definitely a tongue kiss, thus a reminder of the passion she'd once shared with Robby.

"They're in that beginning phase," she offered.

Derrick Mills turned his attention to her once more. "It's amazing how long such a phase can last," he said cheerfully. "My wife and I hope it will go on forever."

It won't, she wanted to ensure. She knew better than these lovesick fools. And between Mr. Hearts-and-Flowers and the two love bunnies in the next room, it was downright hard to conduct this business meeting. "Uh…do you have any more questions to ask?"

Glancing down at the pad on his knee and riffling through the pages, Derrick considered. "Sorry. At any mention of romance, I just…"

Ellie raised a hand and held it up, palm outward. "No need to explain." Sighing, she prompted, "Your next question?"

"I use the old-fashioned stuff," he continued absently. "Paper. The electronic devices drive me crazy. So I'll need just a second to collect my thoughts."

While she waited, Ellie smoothed her skirt and recrossed her ankles. The rust-orange suit and shoes she'd chosen looked amazing, but weren't comfortable. Still, a photographer had arrived with Derrick, and she wanted to seem her best. If a picture did make the paper, Robby would see it, since he always read their popular publication.

Robby. Again! Cutting off the thought, she wondered why the damnable man kept invading her mind. The affair was over. Period. And yet she sometimes awakened, more than she wanted to admit, her sleep-hazy mind full of dreams about the raw sexual passion they'd shared.

"Well," Derrick began. "I believe I've got everything I need. I'm struck by your success. So is my boss. That's why he sent me here. I really wanted to meet you personally, rather than just speak on the phone, and now that I have, I'm truly impressed."

So the article was going to be a good one. She fought the urge to shout with joy. "Thank you, Mr. Mills."

"In under a year you've built an amazing company. You've cut the overhead so much—"

"There's virtually none."

"And many of the clients you previously handled at Lee Polls have remained loyal."

"To me, yes. A lot of…my father's clients followed me, too."

"Any idea why? Robby Robriquet is an excellent and talented manager."

But Robby wasn't bringing home the bacon. He was best with numbers, she with finding new business. Oh, Lee Polls was doing well enough, but she'd been a third of its lifeblood for years. And as far as she knew, her dad really had retired. Not that she'd spoken to him.

"Mr. Robriquet is skilled," she admitted. In fact, in her weaker moments, she hated to see him lose business. She knew how hard he worked, what it meant to him. He was every bit as talented as she, too, but… "The stars were with me."

"Celebrity clients?"

She chuckled. "That, too. On that score, moving to a larger city where I can network more easily has helped. But I meant the stars of fate. I've just had a good run lately."

"You're too modest. You called a few long-shot elections, one national. In fact, so far this year, your polling data has been more accurate than anyone's in the political arena, at any level of politics, local or national. Your analysis has constantly exposed glitches in data, where others have missed them. You've called new trends, too, and that has allowed you to make particularly accurate assessments."

"There was the John Lewis campaign," she agreed, speaking of a senatorial race in the South. "We got lucky there. Then the Wally Willis congressional call. We correctly determined the way Billings Corporation, the pet manufacturer, should drive its new business, as well, which had immediate, positive results for them, and their stock prices soared."

"Results that were nothing short of amazing," he agreed. "Do you care to share your secret?"

She laughed. "You want me to divulge the fine print of my pact with the devil?"

"A lot of people would like to know."

"Just good footwork," she assured him. "Solid data collection and long hours of analyzing numbers."

"A lot of people don't believe that, you know."

She squinted. "Believe what?"

"That you don't have a secret. Your predictions can be downright uncanny in their accuracy. People would pay a small fortune to understand how you do it."

She laughed. "Who? Bookies and weather forecasters?"

"Among others."

"I could tell you about my crystal ball," she joked. "Or the cards I throw. Maybe even the special tricks I use with the I Ching. But I'd be lying. And anyway, starting this business hasn't been a bed of roses."

"Could have fooled the public."

She frowned. "I had some difficulty when I was first getting started. New work was coming in, but…" Robby was still a constant distraction. "I was busy then, helping my friend Susannah Banner open a restaurant in this neighborhood, a sweet little country place named Oh, Susannah's.

"My wife and I eat there all the time, and I knew you and Ms. Banner were friends."

"You've heard of Susannah?"

"In name only. Her husband's famous, and the restaurant's had great reviews. It's wonderful, as I said."

"So is Susannah." Ellie absently lifted a hand, touching the charm she wore. Now she just wished Susannah was in New York. A few days ago, she'd returned to Banner and J.D., after flying in to check on the restaurant. During the visit, she hadn't mentioned Robby, of course, but no doubt, Susannah saw him regularly. Yes…she was treating Ellie with kid gloves, afraid any mention of Robby would send Ellie into a funk. At any rate, Ellie knew Robby and J.D.'s previously shattered relationship had been repaired, so they were pals again, and that meant Susannah was probably often in his company.

So she could have asked about Robby, but somehow she'd

refrained. She didn't want Susannah guessing at her heartbreak and doing the worst possible thing—playing matchmaker.

Derrick Mills was watching her. "Would you like to share anything more, Ms. Lee?"

Ellie thought over the past months, and the mystery surrounding J.D.'s supposed death after an explosive device had been detonated aboard his boat, *The Alabama*. As it turned out, J.D. escaped the wreckage unscathed, but he'd used the opportunity to walk away from his old life and start fresh. By pretending he'd really died, he'd been able to clean up his hard-living ways and win back his wife.

Due to those incidents, Ellie had been forced to return to Banner, however briefly, to attend J.D.'s funeral. It was the last time she'd seen Robby. Even a couple months later, she still felt raw from the experience. He'd looked as good as ever, dressed in a dark suit, and he'd been incredibly kind to Susannah, too, helping her make arrangements, so Ellie couldn't help but feel touched.

She, too, had put aside past animosities. In the brief time they'd spent together, they were thankfully never alone. And they hadn't talked business, nor about their affair, only about Susannah and J.D. Maybe they should have, she thought now. Maybe it would have been better for her and Robby to yell and scream, instead of being civil. Maybe that could have healed the ache that plagued her every time she imagined his face.

The vision of it swam in her mind now. The high forehead, straight nose, full lips. His skin was always glowing from a combination of good health and sun exposure. Swallowing hard, she tried to push away an image of his eyes, but she couldn't. They were sparkling, arresting, deep with knowledge. She and Robby belonged together, Ellie suddenly thought. Every time she thought of him, she knew she'd made a mistake.

Robby was her fate, her destiny. And yet she was powerless to return to him. This office represented her innermost self, too. Even if her parents would fault her for it, work fulfilled her as nothing else could.

Whatever the case, she thought, returning to the topic at hand, Susannah and J.D. were back together, as happy as peas in a pod. "I don't think I want to elaborate on J. D. Johnson and Susannah Banner any more than I already have," Ellie finally decided.

"My only remaining question concerns what you see in your immediate future."

She smiled, thinking the phrase sounded catchy, and making a mental note of it. "The future of Future Trends?" Before he could respond, she continued. "Funny you should ask. I am about to do something totally unprecedented in the history of the polling industry."

Derrick took the bait, leaning forward. "And you're going to let me announce this in my article?"

Astute fellow. "Of course." She flashed a smile. "I'm going to put my money where my mouth is."

"How?"

She glanced toward the front room. "As you've made clear, you're no stranger to the necessity of passion. And ever since Angelina and Antonio became engaged, I've been inspired…"

Now Derrick was beginning to look a little confused.

"By using my polling skills and talents with statistical analysis," she said, "I'm going to find a mate."

Derrick chuckled. "You're kidding, right?"

Slowly, she shook her head. "As you know, today's marketing strategies include tricks unimaginable a generation ago. Today, there are databases chock-full of information about everyone. With nothing more than my computer, I can access a world of data about you—where you go, what you earn, where you shop, what you buy, what you do for entertainment, who you know, what you read…"

"I get the point."

She laughed softly. "Scary thought, isn't it?"

"If misused."

"Well," she assured him, "I'm in the process of putting my data gathering and analytical skills together to demonstrate why everyone should use Future Trends. After this, everyone will understand that we can make any correct prediction, right down to what you're going to have for dinner tonight."

"You're already blowing people out of the water."

"Maybe. But this will be spectacular. Within two weeks, I expect to finish crunching my numbers. In addition to available data, I've requested focus groups and questionnaires, the results to which Angelina is entering into our private database now. And from all the existing information in the country, I expect to find the man with whom I would be the most compatible."

"Of course you intend to meet him before you marry him?" Derrick teased, looking incredulous.

"I would not have to," Ellie assured him. "That's how much I stand behind my methods, but…" Pausing, she shrugged gamely. "I can't expect anyone else to play by my rules, and so…"

"So?"

"The announcement will be made next week."

"And what do you expect to come from this?"

She flashed him a grin. "Besides publicity from you for Future Trends? Mr. Mills, I'm not sure you appreciate the full gravity of what I'm saying. This man will be The One. I will be able to do anything with him…and everything. I can bed him, wed him. Make mad, passionate love. He will be my alter ego and very best friend. That's what I'm looking for, and—"

"My, my," her interviewer interjected. "This is interesting, indeed. Other papers may want to follow this, watch the story unfold."

It was what she'd been hoping for. If things went smoothly, she could actually make a mint in new business, and garner the resources for taking over Lee Polls, if she chose to do so. She took a deep breath. "Let me just finish by saying that I know two things. First, and I speak as a statistician."

"To say?"

"The numbers never lie."

"And…"

"Second, as a woman, I'd say…"

He leaned even closer. "Yes?"

"I always get my man."

He would be better than Robby Robriquet in every way. Sexier. Smarter. Richer. Hotter in bed. And the only remaining question was his identity.

3

DADDY EDDIE *WOULD* pick this booth, Robby thought, sighing as he finished off his burger. As he pushed aside his plate, he stared down to where, years ago, he'd carved his and Ellie's initials into the wood of the table, a practice the proprietor of the Night Rider, Clancy O'Dell, had long encouraged. Blinking, Robby glanced away, adjusting his eyes to the dim interior, the long, ornate bar and mirror, pool table and jukebox.

He paused to survey a photograph signed by his best friend, J. D. Johnson, who was depicted playing his guitar. Ever since he'd become famous as a country-western singer, J.D.'s picture had graced the walls of all the local eateries and businesses, and Robby felt a surge of pride regarding his friend, not to mention relief, since their relationship had gotten back on an even keel. In fact, since J.D. and his wife, Susannah, had reunited, J.D. had come to the Night Rider on weekend nights to play for the locals.

Robby's gaze returned to Daddy Eddie, and he wished it hadn't. Some days, it was damn hard to look at the man, since Ellie was his spitting image. Every glance at the man made him think of Ellie. Just like his daughter, he looked as if he'd recently stepped off the boat from merry ole Ireland. He had the same wavy dark hair that was nearly black in most light, and the same pale, pink-toned skin and blue eyes. The only difference was that Daddy Eddie spent more time in the sun and was covered with freckles. Daddy Eddie's lips were thin and usually pursed, too, while Ellie had been lucky in getting her mama's mouth; she had luscious bee-stung lips she always glossed in pink. Otherwise, she was her father's child, all right, in both looks and temperament.

"The future of Future Trends," spat out Daddy Eddie, his voice exposing a competitive edge as he removed a plaid cap and placed it on the scarred, rough-hewn wood table. Leaning back, he sipped a frothy head off a lager as he continued to study the newspaper article about Ellie.

"'It's easy to see why so many clients have followed Ms. Lee from her father's company. Poised and bristling with intelligence, Ms. Lee is one of those women who has it all. Brains, looks, ambition and a fearless go-getter attitude…'"

Daddy Eddie's voice trailed off as he continued reading, mouthing the words. "Has it all," he muttered, his blue eyes, so like Ellie's, skewering Robby's. "That girl doesn't have jack. She's running an office out of an apartment, for God's sake, and in that degenerate hellhole that some people call New York City. Why, I could have gone there, myself, years ago. But no. I stayed right here in Banner, Mississippi, hiring local people and taking care of my own community."

"You're the biggest employer in the area," Robby agreed, feeling compelled to acknowledge Daddy Eddie's accomplishment. At a time when so many businesses had closed shop in the area, the contribution was even more valued.

"That's right," Daddy Eddie fumed. "I never outsourced, and I never laid off anyone, not even when times were at their toughest and the payroll was hard to meet. My grandpa somehow kept on everybody during the Great Depression. But Ellie? She's run off to the big city now. She'd doesn't give a rat's behind about heritage. And she's scarcely even had a boyfriend, which is downright pathetic at her age. Why, even if she found a man fool enough to date her, she can't so much as boil an egg. Face it, my little girl is ruined."

Pausing, Daddy Eddie shook his head. "You should have seen what happened the last time her mama asked her to help with a pot roast. A simple pot roast! Let me tell you, we had TV dinners that night! And she nearly burnt *them* to a crisp."

"Cooking isn't her strong point," Robby couldn't help but concur. If the truth be told, Ellie wasn't any better at takeout. During their months of bliss, she preferred to lounge around, naked in bed, while Robby got dressed and drove to the Night Rider or the Pizza Palace to pick up victuals. Not that he could tell her father that.

"Even I can make a pot roast," muttered Daddy Eddie. "And I'm a man! Why, when she was at college," Daddy Eddie plunged on, "her mother and I would visit. You know, how parents do?"

Not really, Robby thought, but he nodded dutifully.

"I couldn't believe the boys she introduced to me! Miserable excuses for men! Pure pansies. All of them into art and music and such. Probably even ballet. Tap dancing. Sewing and home economics. You know what I'm saying, Robby?"

"Well," Robby ventured diplomatically. "It's not worth working yourself into a lather about it, Daddy Eddie. You know, you're supposed to watch your blood pressure."

"But you know what I'm saying?" Daddy Eddie demanded. Unfortunately, Robby did. "Uh…yeah."

"A man can't get a grandbaby this way!"

About that, Robby wasn't so sure. He and Ellie had a few scares, mostly because she was so hot and Robby couldn't wait to find a condom. "Give her time," Robby soothed.

Daddy Eddie didn't even hear. "And her brothers are worse! Scoundrels, that's all they are! They always go for the career women, the feminists. Why, absolutely none of my kids will reproduce, and I'm beginning to think it's just to spite me. What did I ever do to them?

"Nothing!" he nearly shouted, answering himself. "Only worked my fingers to the bone, feeding and clothing them. I even got Ellie that convertible car on her sixteenth birthday!"

"You did." She'd looked good in it, too, her hair flying behind her in the wind.

"And for what? To leave my legacy to whom?" Catching Robby's gaze, he quickly amended. "I'm not talking about you running my company. If it weren't for you, Robby, I don't know what I'd do!"

"You know I hang around your sons. It's no secret that if they were more interested in the family business…"

"Dammit," Daddy Eddie muttered under his breath in frustration. "I didn't mean it that way."

Robby let it pass. "Just don't be hard on Ellie," he coached, unable to believe he'd gotten boxed into taking up for her. Somehow, he'd wound up playing the role of go-between in the Lees. However, a million years could pass, and he'd still be stinging from Ellie's parting speech, especially the part when she'd compared him to his father. It was the lowest possible blow and she knew better.

"Why on earth are you defending her?" Daddy Eddie gaped at Robby as if to say he had some nerve. "She's decimated our business, boy. She's used everything I taught her against me, every trick in my bag. Only a man like you could have kept her in line. Yes, maybe a man who acts like a man could have saved her. Made her want to do her duties as a woman. Of course, I can't blame you for never being attracted to my little girl." He blew out a sigh. "Any man in his right mind would steer clear. She's a handful, all right. I wouldn't wish her on any male, no, sir. Certainly not one I respect, such as yourself."

"C'mon," Robby put in quickly, hoping to change the direction of the conversation, "I'm about done with lunch. Why don't you down the rest of that brewski, so we can get out of here? Work calls."

"Can I please have just one more minute in which to finish my lager?" Daddy Eddie snapped, his eyes pinning Robby again. "And by the way, I'm still the only board member at Lee Polls, so I've got a right to speak my mind. I was saying, I suppose there's no possibility of my little girl landing a real man, and this worries me, Robby. First, this country isn't making men like it used to. And second, the girl's too headstrong and selfish, not to mention too damn smart for her own good. And finally, I believe she lacks passion."

Robby's lips parted. "Lacks…passion?"

"Yes. Boys would come along, but she always seemed to chew them up and spit them out. Yes, sir, she used men like bubble gum."

"Who?" Robby was starting to feel testy.

"Well, I don't know all their names."

"I didn't think she was all that serious about guys in college."

"So maybe she didn't sleep with them. Even Ellie's bright enough to know the only point to men is marriage, and the only point to marriage is having babies and carrying on the line."

"That's very old-fashioned."

"Hmm. Believe what you will. And I don't blame you in the least for not wanting to take a more critical look at Ellie. After all, you've had to work with her, and besides—unlike her—you're nice, so you want to give her the benefit of the doubt, as her coworker. My point is she's just not soft and womanly like her mama. I think those feminists turned her off men in college."

Robby winced. "Times *have* changed, Daddy Eddie."

"That's what I keep saying!" Daddy Eddie exploded.

"Ellie's more modern," Robby admitted. "I'll give you that. Still, it doesn't mean she's never going to meet somebody special."

"When?"

"She's not even thirty."

"By the time her mama was thirty, she'd had four kids!"

The defense was starting to sound lame. "True, but nowadays, a lot of women wait longer."

Daddy Eddie squinted, looking wounded and betrayed. "If I didn't know better, I'd think you'd taken a fancy to her, yourself, given the way you come to her defense like some knight in shining armor."

"I'm not defending her," Robby vowed. "I admit she's a little tough." When he thought about some of Ellie's more aggressive moments, he wasn't sure that was necessarily a bad thing, either. "Look, can we talk about something other than Ellie? Let's not ruin our meal, okay?"

"You're finished eating, anyway," countered Daddy Eddie. "And Ellie's the main problem we have today, so she must be dealt with." Glancing down, he shook his head, now reading from the paper once more. "'Showing she can put her money where her mouth is, Ms. Lee is now running the most interesting promotional campaign in the history of the polling business, a move that may well have those at Lee Polls eating their hearts out.'"

Since she'd broken his heart, Robby figured she might as well eat it, too. Again, he said nothing as Daddy Eddie read Ellie's game plan, saying she meant to use her polling skills to find a man.

"Can you imagine?" Daddy Eddie implored, gasping in astonishment.

"No," Robby admitted grimly.

"This proves my point. Love is nothing to her. Nothing!

Why, she'd actually run a poll to find a mate, when we both know that the decision about a life partner is the most important in the world. Classic Ellie," Daddy Eddie declared.

More than he knew. Ellie wasn't just striking at the heart of Lee Polls, but at her ex-lover, too. And ending the affair sure hadn't crimped her style. Every morning, when he looked in the mirror, Robby knew he was worse for wear. His hair was getting streaked with gray and the fine lines around his eyes had deepened, turning into crevices and lending him a weatherworn appearance.

Without Ellie reminding him to eat, he'd lost a few pounds, too, and he was starting to look gaunt. Since he wasn't going to see Ellie at the office, he was letting his stubble grow, only shaving every other day. He'd always hated shaving, anyway.

Ellie, by contrast, looked better than ever. In the picture in the paper, she was wearing a beautiful rust-colored suit he didn't recognize, probably bought for the occasion. Although, no matter what she put on, she looked stunning. Her gray-blue eyes bespoke a strange timelessness, and she had a habit of staring, as if she wasn't at all inclined to blink. Often, when he looked at her, Robby had to force himself to finally look away.

Her body was just as captivating, communicating something eternal. She was tall and long-waisted, in good health, but never muscular, made of sloping curves. Her face was a near-perfect oval, but with a wide forehead, making her look as brainy as heck. In terms of dress, she had the sexy librarian thing down pat.

"Robby?"

He blinked, then damned himself for drifting once more into what he called "the Ellie zone." Often, he'd start thinking about her, only to glance up, look at a clock and realize a full hour had passed. "Huh?"

"I said they're not making men like they used to," Daddy

Eddie continued. "I don't have to tell you that. Do I, Robby?" Before Robby could respond, the man started in once more. "I mean, these fellows I'm talking about, that my little girl used to date in college…why, they'd never even fished or hiked. I ask you, what kind of a fellow can't make his own fish flies?"

"I make mine, so I couldn't say."

"Exactly."

Frequently, Daddy Eddie implied Robby would have made a perfect match for Ellie. However, if he suspected the truth, the man would change his tune in a heartbeat. In fact, Robby's backside would be chock-full of buckshot.

As if reading his mind, Daddy Eddie continued, "And you can sure as hell bet those boys couldn't shoot a gun. What kind of woman would want a man who can't shoot straight?"

That was probably a dangling double entendre, but Robby didn't take the bait. Instead, he abruptly changed the subject. While conversing with Daddy Eddie, one often had to revert to non sequiturs. "I don't really know how to bring this up," Robby said, "but I need to take a few days off."

"Don't we all," crooned Daddy Eddie.

"Sorry you've felt compelled to come back to work, sir," Robby managed. "I do feel bad about it." Suddenly, temper rose inside him. "And dammit," he added, "I'm sorry about the way business is going, Daddy Eddie. I really am. I know you hoped I'd be able to step up to the plate."

"Well, Ellie's got us by the kahunas, son. Mostly because she's female."

There was some truth in it. Some clients had left because she was playing the underdog. Otherwise, her leaving had thrown Robby completely off his game, which didn't help. He felt as deflated as an old birthday balloon. Lee Polls just wasn't the same without her.

Daddy Eddie heaved a sigh. "That's the hell of it, isn't it? Women always have the upper hand. No matter what. And that's the first thing any red-blooded male has to understand about the fairer sex. They rule the world."

"But we have to pretend we do," Robby agreed ruefully, not fully agreeing with Daddy Eddie's point, but having heard this lecture many times.

"Well, maybe you *should* go on vacation."

That was a surprise. "I should?"

Daddy Eddie nodded decisively. "Yes, indeed. You haven't taken a day off since my witchlike daughter so rudely left town." He shook his head in consternation. "She didn't even give two-weeks' notice. Or clean her desk." He eyed Robby. "You and I had to do that, and I know, firsthand, she was raised with better manners than that."

"I just need a couple days."

"Take all the time you want."

"Pardon me for saying so, but why are you trying to get rid of me now?"

Daddy Eddie eyed the newspaper article with a malicious glint in the gaze. "I'd like to be left to my own devices for a few days."

"Great." Long ago, Robby had learned not to trust Daddy Eddie. "What do you have up your sleeve?"

"My plan is still formulating."

"I can't wait to hear." Daddy Eddie could fight just as hard as Ellie. She'd gotten all the man's worst genes. Now God only knew what was brewing in the old coot's devious mind. "Maybe I'd better stick around."

"Oh, you know I wouldn't do anything to hurt Ellie."

"Not lethally," Robby agreed. "That being the case, why don't you share your diabolical plot?"

"Oh, no," Daddy Eddie said with a sudden, soft chuckle

that didn't bode well in Robby's humble opinion. "You need to clear your head, so you'd better go on vacation. In fact, why don't you take the rest of the day off to organize your things?"

Hearing a ruckus behind him, and feeling half glad for the interruption, Robby glanced over his shoulder toward the door, just in time to see Max Sweeney cross the threshold. In a heartbeat, blind fury claimed Robby and pure killer instinct took over.

Daddy Eddie's attention sharpened, too. "Bastard," he muttered simply.

"That guy always makes me see red."

Sweeney was definitely a weasel. Short and slight of build, he was pale-skinned, with a face constructed entirely of points—a sharp chin, beak nose, jutting cheekbones. Everybody knew he collected bets on races, but Sheriff Kemp had never caught him red-handed. Sweeney was no stranger to Robby, either. And now he tried not to think of how, years ago, Max would corner Robby's old man, Charlie, in the Night Rider and ply him with booze, wearing down his resistance. Once Charlie couldn't think straight, Max would get him to bet on various sports games. Horses, cars, football, you name it.

Then, when Charlie lost, there was no way to pay Max, since Max had already encouraged Charlie to spend his paycheck on booze. So then Max would turn around and demand exorbitant interest on whatever Charlie owed.

To add insult to injury, Max, himself, had a son only a few years older than Robby on whom Max had doted. Johnny Sweeney had the good grace not to look like his father, too, and some of the stupider girls around the surrounding bayous had fallen for him. The fact that he was always flush with cash helped.

Max had given his only son everything. He'd driven late model, high-end cars since he'd gotten a license, and he'd gone to top-of-the-line schools, both prep and college. He'd experienced a life of travel and privilege, and now he was a lawyer, practicing part-time in a nearby town called Sunset Bayou.

"Damn loan shark," Daddy Eddie spat out with displeasure, speaking of Max.

Robby merely shrugged. What he wouldn't do to bring the guy down, though. He wasn't defending his old man, of course. The instinct was purely selfish. Sweeney belonged behind bars, if only for the nights Robby had gone hungry after he'd gotten Charlie Robriquet to squander the rent and grocery money.

If it hadn't been for Patricia Lee, Ellie's mother and Daddy Eddie's wife, Robby figured he would have starved to death. To this day, he was fairly certain Daddy Eddie had no idea how many times his wife had come calling at the shack Charlie and Robby had called home. Always, she'd drop off leftovers or an "extra" pie she'd made.

Not that Robby had minded taking her charity. He'd once heard Daddy Eddie say that Patricia Lee's smile could take the sting out of a bumblebee and that was the truth. She was, by far, the nicest, most maternal woman Robby had ever met. Sighing, he acknowledged once again that his ex-lover had gotten Daddy Eddie's genes, not Patricia's.

And that's what drove Robby so crazy. Ellie was unpredictable, fiery and determined in everything she attempted, and Robby could never quite let go of the challenge....

Suddenly, his ears pricked up. At the bar, Clancy was showing Max the article about Ellie. Just the thought of the weasel's eyes on a picture of Ellie made Robby's blood boil. When he heard Max's insinuating voice, his fingers curled into a fist.

"She sure knows how to call 'em," Max said, his high-pitched, nasal voice traveling. "Knowledge like hers would sure come in handy at a racetrack." He chortled. "Not that I'm a gambling man."

"It's a good thing my daughter uses her talents for nobler causes," Daddy Eddie called, raising his voice just enough to be heard over the jukebox, which was now playing one of J. D. Johnson's songs. The tune was a slow, soul-wrenching love song that only served to remind Robby of Ellie.

"Oh, Eddie," returned Max. "Hey, there. I didn't see you."

"Look before you leap," Daddy Eddie suggested.

Max arched an eyebrow. "Did I say something to offend you? Why, I figured you'd feel proud to see your daughter in a big-city newspaper like that."

But Max had said Ellie's talents might be useful to him. "I'm proud of my daughter," Daddy Eddie returned, "whether she makes the papers or not."

Fortunately, Max was only getting a six-pack to go, and as soon as Clancy bagged the brews, Robby figured he'd be out the door. No such luck. Once he'd shoved the bag under his arm, Max sauntered toward them and stopped in front of the table.

"A lot's going on around here, eh? Ellie's her daddy's own competitor now?" he said conversationally. "And last time I was down at Delia's Diner, listening to the gossip, I heard Robby's got some exciting news, himself."

Robby said nothing. All his senses were on heightened alert, and maybe if he was lucky, he would manage not to rise and throttle the man. Already, he was imagining the pleasure of contact when his fist pummeled Max Sweeney's jaw. He could hear the crack, the ugly split of flesh, feel a trickle of blood. "What do you want, Max?"

"Just starting a conversation," Max said innocently.

"Well, I think Robby just finished it," said Daddy Eddie.

"I'm being neighborly," attested Max. "And I figured he must be feeling good today. In fact, I figured maybe you two were having lunch to celebrate."

The weasel was referring to Charlie's homecoming next

week. After eight years in jail for manslaughter, Robby's father was finally being released. "Why do you always try to talk to me about my old man, Max?" Robby found himself challenging, his low voice controlled and scarcely audible over the sound of one of the jukeboxes. "I mean, you never did either of us any favors. So what's it to you?"

"Just being neighborly, like I said. A man's got to care about his community."

What hogwash. Luckily, the door swung open again, and a slice of autumnal light cut across the linoleum floor of the bar. For a second, despite the circumstances, Robby almost smiled, since J. D. Johnson had appeared in the open doorway, backlit by the sun, which threw him into silhouette. He sported a thin white shirt, despite the day being cool for October in Mississippi, and he wore threadbare jeans, boots and a Stetson hat. "Looks like my gunslinger friend just showed up," Robby said. "So why don't you get lost, Sweeney."

Taking the hint, the man turned away, passing J.D. as he came toward Robby and Daddy Eddie's table, with his wife, Susannah, right behind him. Over his shoulder, Max called, "I'll be wishing the best for your family, Robby."

"Bastard," muttered J.D., standing in front of the booth, exactly where Max had been just a moment before.

"That's what I said," returned Daddy Eddie. Then, "Hi, Susannah. Sorry you had to hear the rough language, sweetheart."

"Nothing I don't hear from J.D. at home."

"Hey, Suze," said Robby.

She smiled, and when she did, it brought Robby a whole new wave of heartbreak, recalling the good times he and Ellie had hanging around J.D. and Susannah. Why, Ellie and Susannah had been inseparable from birth, and although Ellie was doing well in New York, Robby couldn't help but imagine she wouldn't be happier back at home in Banner. Face it, he thought now, she'd be a fish out of water in the city. Successful, but without her family and friends.

Nowadays, Susannah always made things worse for Robby—always talking about how good Ellie looked, how happy she was working for herself, and how she seemed to secretly miss him, something Robby very much doubted.

"Hey, stranger," Susannah said, ruffling Robby's hair.

"Careful," he warned, catching her hand.

"Afraid I'll make your girlfriends jealous?" she teased.

"That or your husband," said J.D.

Robby rolled his eyes. He had no girlfriends. Everybody knew that, and most, except Patricia and Daddy Eddie, knew why, too. Ellie had left him in the dirt because he'd ascended the ranks at Lee Polls.

"Hey, there," he said on a sigh. "Pull up a chair, you two, although I warn you, Daddy Eddie and I are headed back to work soon."

"We're only here for takeout," Susannah explained. "In fact, if you two can occupy J.D., I'll head to the bar and see if our call-in order is ready."

Robby grinned, glancing at the friend he'd known since grade school. "Is J.D. bothering you again, Susannah? Maybe I ought to beat him up for you."

Before she could answer, J.D. had circled his wife's waist, hauled her against his side, angled his head down and delivered a sloppy kiss. Giggling, she said, "See how he treats me!"

"Always having his way with you," Robby agreed. "He deserves punishment, no doubt."

"She loves it," protested J.D.

"Well, all your lovin' *has* left me as hungry as a horse," Susannah said, whirling and offering her backside as she headed for the bar.

"Helluvu woman," J.D. complimented his wife, tilting back his Stetson and grinning.

"Don't rub it in," Robby complained.

"Yes, Robby works too damn hard," Daddy Eddie put in. "He needs to find himself a woman."

"That so," J.D. said with a wry grin.

Taking a deep breath, Robby met J.D.'s eyes over the head of the older man, reminding him to keep mum. Yeah, Robby figured it would be best if Daddy Eddie never guessed at his private life. Determined not to be the focus, Robby quickly introduced the hot topic around town, the budding relationship between Sheriff Kemp and Delia, which gave the men a few minutes of mileage.

Then, of course, the topic rolled around to Robby again. "Maybe he'll go somewhere hot and steamy on his vacay," said Daddy Eddie.

"A desert island?" queried J.D.

"Wherever he can find a woman."

"Hmm, I could use one of those," Robby finally offered in a noncommitted tone.

"Wait. You're going womanizing, and you didn't invite me?" J.D. joked.

"I heard that," Susannah called, blowing a lock of blond hair from her eyes as she came up behind J.D. with the bag containing their food order.

"Caught in the act," said J.D.

Susannah smirked. "You know I'm the only woman fool enough to have you."

J.D. shot her a bad-boy grin. "So true."

"We'd better go while the food's hot," she added.

"Nope," he corrected, "we'd better go, since I'm thinking you're so hot."

Scoffing, she said goodbye. Then J.D. offered a few parting

words. When the couple was gone, Robby realized they'd left nothing but heartache in their wake. Dammit, for a brief while, he and Ellie had shared their closeness. Oh, he'd wanted Ellie all her life, ever since he'd first seen her, but he'd also known how much Daddy Eddie and Patricia had doted on their only girl. Especially Daddy Eddie, who tried to cover up his unstoppable devotion by being hard on her. How, Robby had wondered, could he ever become a worthwhile suitor?

Ellie had deserved so much more. A good-looking college man from a loving home. By contrast, Robby was the son of a man who couldn't put clothes on his kid's back, or food on the table, a rowdy town drunk with a gambling problem.

That was why he'd done all he could to steer clear of Ellie. For years, he'd worked his tail off, still did. He'd taken gifts from Daddy Eddie to get through school, but since then, he'd insisted on paying the money back. Daddy Eddie hadn't wanted to take the money, but he'd done so in the end, after Robby threatened to leave Lee Polls if he didn't.

Now his throat felt raw and tight. He wasn't proud of it, but emotion was getting the best of him. Maybe things were better this way, he decided. Maybe Ellie would find a man in New York who'd had all the advantages and grown up without knowing want. A guy like Johnny Sweeney. The thought came from nowhere, and now Robby pushed it away, ashamed of himself for making such comparisons, especially since the other man's father was even worse than Charlie, in Robby's humble opinion.

"Why so deep in thought?" Daddy Eddie prompted.

"You should have promoted Ellie, not me," Robby abruptly said.

Daddy Eddie's jaw dropped. "Lord, you really do need a vacation. And don't you ever second-guess me, son," he said. "The company's been in my family since the eighteen hundreds, so I figure I know what's best for it."

But couldn't Daddy Eddie see? Without Ellie in his bed, Robby had fallen apart. Sales and contracts were tanking. It wasn't dire, they weren't going to lose the business, but... Blowing out a frustrated sigh, he tried not to think about how Ellie's desertion had thrown him off his game. Worse, she wasn't the least bit affected.

He just couldn't think straight. It was as if some necessary hormone inside him had been depleted. Yeah, he thought now, testosterone. "I really do need to take a couple days off," he said again.

When he glanced up, Daddy Eddie was studying him. "I know what this is all about. Are you going to pick up your dad?"

"From prison?" Robby was stunned at the idea. He'd been thinking about Ellie and hadn't bothered to give Charlie a second thought, but his father was being released in a few days. "Hell, no," he exploded. "The man got himself arrested and put in prison, he can leave by himself, too."

Daddy Eddie considered a long moment, then tilted his head, looking undecided about what he should say. "He may have changed. Eight years is a long time."

Robby clenched his jaw. Men like his father never changed. He'd learned that a long time ago. So many nights, he'd lain in bed, wondering if he'd awaken to sirens and find Sheriff Kemp on the porch with bad news. No matter what Robby had done—acted out, yelled at Charlie, tried to reason—nothing had worked.

"You don't know him like I do."

"Maybe not, but I've seen people change," offered Daddy Eddie.

"Who?"

There was a long pause.

"That's what I thought," Robby commented.

Daddy Eddie sighed. "I know you hate it when I tell you

this, but your daddy was a good man. He doted on your mama. And when she died, when you were little, he was just broken-hearted. He couldn't go on."

Despite having a son? Robby wanted to challenge. Dammit, Charlie had had responsibilities, a boy at home. "Even if he's changed, somehow, it's water under the bridge to me." Robby had grown up a long time ago.

"You can't give him a chance?"

"What?" Robby scoffed. "Pick him up at the jail? Set him up in an apartment or something?" He shook his head adamantly. "Let the system take care of that. I pay taxes. That's all I'm doing. I figure he's got a parole officer to help him. Whatever."

Even saying the words, he felt a rush of guilt, then hated himself for it, not to mention Max Sweeney, and then Daddy Eddie, for bringing up the topic. Oh, Charlie wasn't a bad man, particularly. Robby knew what Daddy Eddie was trying to say. He was, however, a weak man, and the weak could be dangerous. Yes…what was that saying? Never underestimate the power of the blind and stupid, Robby thought. Well, that summed up his father to a T.

Recollections suddenly flooded Robby's mind, of the night his father had killed a beautiful young teenager named Shirley Fey. For some reason that no one had ever discerned, she was out walking late one night, near the cabin Charlie and Robby had shared. She'd been found dead on the road, victim of a hit and run. Charlie hadn't even bothered to come forward. Later, he claimed he'd been so drunk he barely remembered what he'd done.

Shirley Fey hadn't deserved it. She'd been from a family that was almost as poor, a thin girl, almost waifish, with waist-long honey hair. It had nearly killed him, but Robby attended all the legal proceedings, not to stand by his father, but to judge him, right along with the Feys.

Now, for the umpteenth time, Robby vowed never to so much as look at his father again. Charlie could rot in hell, along with devils like Max Sweeney. Ellie, too, he suddenly thought. More than anybody, she damn well knew not to compare him to his old man. What had gotten into her that morning?

"You okay, Robby?"

"He didn't even stop his car that night," Robby murmured. "Maybe she was still alive after he hit her. Maybe she could have been saved."

Daddy Eddie shook his head. "That whole series of events never sat right with me. I know you don't like me saying so, but the trial just moved too fast, and Charlie must have changed his story ten times."

"Quit trying to make me feel better about having a scumbag for a dad," Robby warned. Daddy Eddie and Patricia had always insisted on smoothing the edges off Robby's rough beginnings. By the time they were done discussing Charlie, a stranger would have assumed he was a saint. It was the Lees' way of trying to help.

"I changed my mind," Robby said now. "I'm going to stick around and work. No vacay."

"Why?"

Because he'd just be left with spare time on his hands, and if the past months were any indication, he'd only use it to torture himself with how he'd lost Ellie. "Too much work to do." And he'd prefer not to dwell on his father.

"All right…" Daddy Eddie picked up the newspaper and tapped the picture of his daughter. "Since you've decided to stick around, maybe it's time we came up with a plan for showing Ellie who's boss. We've got to get our clients back, at least. And it'd be nice to find a way to buy Ellie's company…maybe make her think it's another buyer. In fact, since you were talking about taking a trip, maybe you should pay her a visit."

As if. Robby wasn't about to get directly involved in Daddy Eddie's corporate vendetta with his daughter. He was damned if he did, damned if he didn't. If he succeeded at work, he helped himself and Eddie, but hurt Ellie, and he was starting to feel downright paralyzed.

"Yes, sir," Daddy Eddie ventured. "I think I've got it now, and I'm sure I can talk you into helping me. Don't you want to see Ellie get what she deserves for deserting Lee Polls?"

"Uh...sure. Of course I do."

"Then hear me out."

Robby shrugged. "Do I have a choice?"

"Nope," replied the older man.

And then, before Robby could protest again, Daddy Eddie began laying out the master plan about how to deal with his daughter—and Robby's ex-lover.

4

EVERY TIME ELLIE tried to push away a mental image of Robby, so she could concentrate on the man walking her home, she found it impossible. Robby's sculpted face would swim before her eyes, those sparkling baby blues lustily assessing her body while his full lips parted as if for a soul-shattering kiss. Oh, what she wouldn't give to feel that man's hot, rock-hard body pressed against hers just one more time, but of course, that was impossible.

"Well…uh…I mean, it sure is weird, isn't it?"

The voice coming from beside her drew Ellie from her reverie, and she forced herself not to shudder when she glanced at Percy Anders. Or down at him, more precisely, since he would have still been a good five inches shorter than she, even if she weren't wearing black spike heels. "Weird?"

"Yes, weird. You and me, getting together like this."

"Yes…it certainly is," she managed to say, not slowing her steps, her heels beating a fast tattoo on the sidewalk. In fact, it was the understatement of the century, and Ellie had no idea what on earth to do now that she'd met her supposed dream man. *This just can't be happening,* she thought, trying not to gape at her companion.

"Slow down," he said. "If I didn't know better, I'd think you were trying to run away."

"Sorry," she managed.

"I didn't disappoint, did I?"

What could she say to that? "Absolutely not."

But what had gone wrong? She was brilliant, after all. Worthy of running Lee Polls and creating Future Trends. She'd flawlessly anticipated election results and buying patterns of countless consumers. Word of mouth preceded her most places she went, a major paper had made her business a focus, and her skills were sought by those who needed to predict accurate results. She was one of the best in her field. Her ex-lover and her own father were her only competition.

But now…she must have lost the Midas touch. Or some strange twist of fate had skewed her results. She just wished it wasn't quite so quiet and desolate outside this evening, but it was October, which meant it was starting to get dark early. Even cabs seemed scarce on the street. Occasionally, she noticed a carved pumpkin in a window, but otherwise, there were no signs of life. In New York, she always found such silence creepy. Elsewhere, such as in Banner, one expected to encounter lonely stretches of roadway, but never in New York City.

Worse, her sidekick was…just that. If they were attacked, she'd have to come to her own defense, that much was certain. Once more, Robby invaded her thoughts. This time, she found herself imagining his broad shoulders and muscular chest. Yes, he could be quite the defender. A natural-born protector. She envisioned him as he looked when going fishing.

He'd always looked so competent wading into water when he fished, which was one of his passions. She could just see him, the rubber boots hugging his muscular thighs, a long, practiced arm reaching back with a rod to cast the line. Yes…if the world as they knew it ever came to an end, he was exactly the kind of guy who'd know how to rise to the occasion. He could hunt, fish, build fires and cook his catch. Sighing, she shook her head to empty it of the images.

Well, she thought, hopefully Percy A... take advantage of their isolation tonight a... vile, such as attempt to kiss her. Her hand tigh... her evening bag as she continued to walk. Maybe... brain him with it, or offer a swift kick to his shin with... her spike heels. Surely, that would cripple him. As it was, uncomfortable shoes were certainly cramping her own feet.

And for what? she fumed now, trying not to think of the hours she'd spent dressing for their abysmal date. Worse, she'd just seen that unmistakable sexual male glint in the man's eyes, and she intended to stave off any misguided intimacy however she could. Once more, she clutched her bag. Given how she felt about Percy Anders, she doubted she'd stop shy of murder if he tried anything.

Nevertheless, it was she who had begun this charade, wasn't it? Yes, this was all her fault. Now she had to end the relationship before it began, but there was no way to back out gracefully. Surely, she could think of something. She had to. Maybe she could pay him to go away…or to fake his death….

"I just can't believe our luck," he continued, now gingerly placing a hand under her elbow. The gesture made her wish she hadn't worn her fanciest shawl over a short-sleeved, black cocktail dress, since the touch of his sweaty palm against her bare skin was enough to make her shiver.

"Hmm," she murmured, not even wanting to attempt to converse. Oh, it was uncharitable, but she was stunned. She'd followed all her formulas, crunched all the data, and her fantasies had been conclusive.

Angelina had clocked just as many hours as Ellie, entering numbers into the computer. For a while, Ellie's assistant had been so excited that she'd seemed to cease to think about her own wedding. "You're going to find a man!" Angelina had enthused, her voice bubbling.

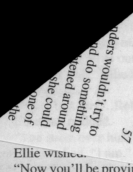

llie had assured her.

ke Antonio and me!"

lf as hot as the one I broke

"he'll be worth all the work

Bride

nders wouldn't try to
d do something
tened around
she could
ne of
the

57

Ellie wished.

"Now you'll be proving your business acumen and getting wined and dined all at the same time," Angelina had said, grinning. "This guy is going to be a keeper."

On the phone, even Susannah had been supportive, urging Ellie to move on from her thoughts about Robby. If Ellie didn't know better, she'd think Susannah was trying to use reverse psychology—in an attempt to make Ellie approach Robby and make up with him. But Susannah had sworn she was sincere. "This guy is going to be ten times better than Robby Robriquet," she'd declared. "I can feel it in my bones, Ellie."

"Remember the time," Ellie had reminisced, laughing, using their pet phrase whenever a significant new memory was in the process of being made.

Now Ellie didn't know what to do. She'd expected Percy Anders to be as good-looking as Robby, at least. Or as sexy, or smart, or educated. Even as rich. Anything. But as near as she could tell, Percy Anders had absolutely nothing to recommend him—harsh, but true. Tonight had been the grimmest date she'd ever endured, and even worse, she'd had to pretend she'd been enjoying it because reporters had shown up. As per your own request, she reminded herself now, hating the box into which she'd put herself.

"Cold?" he ventured.

"No!" she defended, maybe too adamantly, worried he'd misread her shivers and use the excuse to put his arm around her.

"Now, don't snap at me, Ellie," he chided.

"Sorry," she bit out.

"You did shiver."

"A lot of people shiver," she replied.

"Hmm. Only if they're cold. Or if they're…"

Aroused. *Oh, no,* she thought. "I'm fine! Really! Not cold, nor…uh, you know!"

"Well, I don't know if I mentioned it," he said conversationally, "but my horoscope said something truly unexpected was going to happen to me that would change my whole life, and now I guess it has."

Great. "Yes…but horoscopes aren't something I completely trust."

"Maybe not. Though for a guy like me to have a woman like you waltz into his life—"

"I wouldn't get too invested in this…" She couldn't bring herself to utter the word *relationship* since there wasn't one. Nor was one going to develop. Speeding her steps, she sighed in relief when the door to her brownstone came into sight. She just wished Angelina had been working late, so she'd have a better excuse to ditch Percy at the door, but the windows to the apartment were pitch-black, and she'd forgotten to leave on the porch light.

Maybe it was wishful thinking, but for a second, she could have sworn she heard someone behind her and Percy. She wrenched around. No one. Why did it feel as if eyes had settled on her back? Maybe because it was almost Halloween. Ghosts and scarecrows were everywhere. As the hair at her nape prickled, she fought back another shiver.

"Are you okay?"

"Fine."

"You seem a little nervous."

"It's our first date. What do you expect?" Unfortunately, it wasn't to be their last little get-together. Silently, she damned herself for making a big deal out of using her skills to find her "dream man." Yes, as soon as she'd first laid eyes on Percy, when he'd come to pick her up this evening, she'd known something had gone terribly wrong. But what? Her mind reeled, reviewing her strategy and going over her calculations. In her life, she'd never been so sure of an accurate prediction.

Maybe it was true. Maybe Percy Anders was her dream man. And yet it simply couldn't be. *When you reach the front door,* she coached herself now, *be quick.* She'd mutter a thank-you for the wonderful evening, then she'd back inside and shut the door.

Yes, five more minutes and this grisly first date with her dream man would be over. Thankfully, the reporters who'd shown up tonight had already gone home, and since Ellie had chosen to go to Susannah's restaurant, the date had been a little more bearable. She knew the waitstaff, so she'd been surrounded by familiar faces, at least.

"I'm totally invested in our relationship," Percy said, picking up the earlier thread of conversation. "Not just because you're so pretty, either, Ellie. I read all about your polling skills, so I know how smart and accurate you are. That means you must be right about us.

"What you did was a big gamble, Ellie, and I like a woman who takes risks." He paused. "I mean, it's no accident that you're so good with numbers and I'm an accountant."

Stopping in her tracks, Ellie blew out a long sigh as she turned to face Percy. As she looked at him, everything inside her froze. Then guilt rushed in. She felt a little sorry for him, and once more admitted he was creepy, but not dangerous or malicious. He came up to her chin, and once she'd readjusted her gaze, she let her eyes drift over him.

Her heart squeezed with pity once more, since he looked terribly uncomfortable in a new-looking suit he'd probably bought for this dinner. Unbidden, another image of Robby entered her mind. This time, her ex-lover was clad in the chocolate slacks and sport coat he'd been wearing before the first time they'd made love. Robby always made clothes look good. He was frugal, and Ellie doubted he spent much on what he wore, but on him, fabrics flowed and everything looked custom made.

By contrast, in a navy pinstripe, Percy Anders looked comical. The shoulder seams hit an inch beneath his shoulders, the waist button was too tight, the pants a smidgeon long, drooping over oxford-style shoes. His hair, what there was of it, since he was going bald, had just been cut. Light wisps of brown were combed carefully over the scalp, as if that might fool her into thinking he had more hair than he actually did. And his glasses—round, gold, wire frames—kept slipping downward on a tiny nose.

Maybe she was being hard on him. After all, Robby Robriquet was a hunk. Few men could pass muster by comparison. "Listen, Percy," she began diplomatically. "This really is an odd situation…"

Looking encouraged, he lifted a hand and settled it on her shoulder, making her realize her mistake. Why hadn't she kept heading for her apartment as they walked? They were only a few doors away now.

"More than odd," he said. "I've never heard of a woman conducting a poll to find a man."

"It may well be the first time in the history of the world," she admitted, wondering what on earth she'd been thinking.

"And aren't you glad you did?"

He seemed hopeful…and she had to play this game a while, at least until the media lost interest. Otherwise, it would be an admission of defeat and Future Trends might suffer the consequences. "Sure. The thing is," she continued, "it is an unusual circumstance, so I'm sure you agree we need to take things slow." Just in case he didn't understand the full measure of what she was saying, she repeated with emphasis, "Very slow."

"No kiss good-night?"

Before she thought it through, she'd almost pivoted on her heel and run for the door. Her heart hammered in horror at the possibility, but somehow she managed a tight smile and started walking again. "I don't think so," she insisted. "Not tonight."

"I can see your point," he said, sounding disappointed.

She hoped her extreme relief wasn't visible. "Good."

"But we will be seeing each other soon?"

What choice did she have? Besides, they'd already discussed a future date over dinner. "Of course."

"Should we set the exact time now?"

Don't call us, we'll call you. "Because it's something of a promotional thing…"

"Promotional?"

"Well, reporters are aware of it."

"They won't be tagging along next time, will they?"

"I'm afraid so."

"I understand."

Clearly, he didn't. Ellie felt another rush of pity, then guilt, then a burst of anger at Robby. If the fool man hadn't betrayed her, none of this would be happening. Clamping her lips together, she sucked a breath through her nostrils. It was a good thing she hadn't seen Robby in a while.

Men, she thought. They were nothing but trouble. All of them, including Percy Anders. Thankfully, she and her companion were heading up the steps to her apartment now, and the night could be brought to a close. "I appreciate your seeing me home," she said curtly.

"I'd better walk you all the way inside."

"There's no need," she assured him, digging into her bag for the keys. Squinting, she silently berated herself for not turning on the porch light earlier. "There," she said when she found the lock.

"Really," repeated Percy. "Before I go, I want to make sure you're inside, safe and sound."

She had to admit he was doing his best to play the gentleman. "Thanks," she forced herself to say as he followed her into the hallway of the building. Reaching, she snapped on the overhead, and when she turned, wished the light wasn't quite so glaring. All lit up, Percy looked starstruck. If any doubt remained that the man had a serious crush on her, it ended when his eyes skated hungrily over her dress.

"Well, thank you," she afforded, shifting to open the door to her apartment proper.

Taking the hint, he put his hand on the knob of the lobby door. "You'll call me soon?"

"As soon as I can take a look at my calendar," she assured him. She'd call the reporter Derrick Mills, too. At least he could come along as an unwitting chaperone. Fighting rising heat in her cheeks, she tried not to recall the quizzical look on Derrick's face tonight when he'd arrived, along with a few fellow reporters, to meet them at Oh, Susannah's and get quotes for his follow-up story.

"Don't wait too long, Ellie," Percy said. "I know it's only our first date, but…"

Feeling pretty sure she didn't want to hear the rest, she braced herself. "But?"

"You're the best thing that's ever happened to me."

Her lips parted, and she was just about to deny it, then she said, "I'm glad you feel that way, Percy."

She could see the man's throat working as he swallowed, as if around a lump. "I mean it," he continued.

"I know you do."

"No...let me finish. Just being around a woman as beautiful and accomplished as yourself has helped restore my confidence. I...well, let's say if I never did see you again, Ellie, my life would have changed because of tonight."

This was really too much. "Please," she managed. "Don't give me so much power. I'm sure you're exaggerating to make me feel good."

He shook his head adamantly. "I haven't liked the direction in which my life is going lately, Ellie, and you've reminded me of that. Today, just getting ready for our date, I went to the gym for the first time in ages. And instead of procrastinating, the way I've been doing, I finished some unpleasant tasks."

Once more, Ellie found herself sizing up her companion. No...he wasn't dangerous, but he was very lonely and needy. Once more, she wondered what had happened with her polling data. She'd crunched the numbers more than once. Had Angelina made an error while entering information from the questionnaires? She shook her head. No, Angelina was obsessed with her upcoming wedding, but she'd always been careful. Previously, she'd never made any errors.

"I want you to know how I feel," Percy went on. "How important you are to me already."

"Maybe it's time we called it a night, Percy," Ellie suggested softly, trying to be nice.

"Oh, sorry," he said quickly. "I know you must be tired."

"Good night."

"Night," he returned.

A moment later, he was gone and she was inside her own apartment. Leaning, she pressed her back against the door and took a deep breath. Surely, Percy Anders was not a correct match....

A sudden rush of pique overcame her. The cameraman who'd come with Derrick Mills had taken photographs of her and Percy. What if the newspaper did a follow-up story carrying them? She wasn't proud of it, but she'd positively die if Robby saw her with Percy. It would have the exact opposite effect of what she'd intended.

"Which was?" she muttered, now furious at herself. Not to make him jealous, she decided. After all, she'd never take him back, not even if he showed up on his knees. She'd felt belittled by what Robby had done, though, and she supposed she wanted to give him a taste of his own medicine. And like it or not, she was competitive.

"It's my worst flaw," she said on a sigh. So she'd wanted Robby to know she was supersuccessful and looked better than ever. On that score, the first picture in the newspaper had been perfect.

If only she'd had a dazzling hunk by her side, she'd thought when she'd seen it. Once she found her dream mate, Robby would know she'd moved on. Now the plan had backfired, since Percy was hardly what she'd had in mind. Slowly, unable to believe how things were unfolding, she shook her head. "What have I gotten myself into?" she whispered.

And more important, how was she going to get herself out of it?

SO THIS WAS WHAT BEING on cloud nine felt like, Percy thought, shoving his hands deep into his pockets as he practically floated through the soft, slightly chilly night. Immediately, he frowned, feeling troubled since Ellie had chosen to live on such an unsavory block of the Lower East Side. Oh, the section of Manhattan had become trendy lately, and no doubt a Realtor had pushed the area. And, yes, the rents were better than uptown, but Ellie deserved the very best…Fifth Avenue, red carpets, dazzling lights.

"But she likes you just the way you are," he murmured. He could tell. Yes, for Ellie, he wouldn't have to put on airs, or wish he had more money. He was always worried about not providing well enough for a woman. But Ellie was so nice. Her friend, Susannah, too, he imagined as he continued a few blocks, now passing the restaurant where he and Ellie had dined. The food had been excellent. Ellie would know just where to go and what to order. "She's so sophisticated," he whispered.

And he was the man for her. Imagine! Statistics did not tell a lie. Too bad she hadn't let him kiss her good-night, but their physical intimacy was sure to begin soon. He could just tell. A lot of women were shy, and he couldn't blame them in the least, especially not a class act like Ellie. He'd bet a lot of men had come on to her in the past.

Glancing around, he decided he might as well walk home, rather than catch a cab, since his condo was in Battery Park City. It was only a half hour's walk. "It's too good to be true," he said. "We live practically next door to each other."

When he'd first received the call explaining the poll Ellie had conducted, he'd been dubious, of course. Any man would have been. Besides, luck wasn't exactly his middle name. Then the truth had sunk in and his spirits had soared. Ever since, Percy had felt as if he'd won the lotto.

"Everything's going to change now." He was going back to the gym again tomorrow. He'd gotten soft and flabby, and surely Ellie wouldn't like that. She wasn't superficial, so what a man looked like wouldn't affect Ellie Lee much; still, he wanted her to have the best, and that included a man who was in tip-top shape.

Come tomorrow, he was back in action, work-wise, too. Yeah, he was going to turn himself into a real heavy hitter—

getting all the new clients and boning up on out-of-state tax laws so he'd be cooking next tax season. Being an accountant wasn't the world's most exciting work, at least he'd never thought so, but it sure wouldn't hurt him to become more aggressive. He could start to consider other professions, too.

Face it, he'd become an accountant because his father had been one, his grandfather, too. With Ellie's moral support, he could take some night classes and go into something that would interest him more. Architecture had been his passion, but no one had bothered to encourage it. With a woman like Ellie, though, anything was possible.

"I just can't believe it," he sighed, shaking his head. Recently, he'd flat-out rejected his assistant, Helen Wharton, at the office. Thinking about the incident, he felt guilt overtake him. Since coming to work for him a year ago, Helen had become attracted to him. She was awfully nice, too. Pretty in her own way, with curly brown hair and a figure some would call plump, but that he called curvy. She had sweet brown eyes that were usually too shy to meet his and favored demure skirts and sweater sets that turned him on.

Until last week, he'd just guessed at her feelings. But then, she'd come right out and asked him to the movies.

He'd rejected her immediately.

"Oh, I'm so sorry, Percy," she'd said, apologizing. "I know I work for you, so I never should have asked. But I just thought you might like…" Her voice had trailed off.

"No problem," he'd said. "But you're right. We do work together." Then, seeing the stricken look on her face, he'd added, "Don't worry about it. I'm flattered."

Her relief had been visible. "Let's just forget I asked, okay?"

"Absolutely," he'd concurred.

But he hadn't rejected her due to the coworker relationship, he admitted now, feeling a wave of self-loathing. If the truth be told, he was so worried sweet Helen would discover his dirty little habit. After all, she was so efficient and proactive, wanting to please him, and she was always fussing around his desk, straightening papers and organizing folders.

Which, of course, meant he lived in terror regarding what she might find. That was why he'd always been more abrupt with her than necessary, hoping to drive her away, but his surliness had seemed to have the opposite effect. Now things were worse. Helen was pussyfooting around him, walking on eggshells, and that made him hate himself all the more.

Suddenly, he raised his chin. What had captured his attention? He looked right, then left. Seeing nothing out of the ordinary, he turned down Houston Street, then one of the side streets through Soho and wended toward the Hudson, since his apartment was near the water. A horn sounded behind him.

"Oh, no," he muttered, turning in time to see a dark sedan pulling beside him. His heart beat double time. "Please, don't let it be Jimmy C. and Joey D." He didn't know the last names of either man, only the initials associated with their surnames, and that they worked for Big Frank. "I said I'd call them," he whispered as the car drew closer to the curb. Should he run? No…he was out of shape. He wouldn't get far.

When the car stopped, Percy froze, watching the driver-side window power down. "Hey, guys," he managed as the passenger-side door opened like the wing of a dark bird and Jimmy C. got out. The man stared at him over the hood of the car.

"Look what we've got here, Joey," Jimmy said.

"I see," Joey returned from inside the car.

Both men were burly and had fairly dark complexions, but Joey was the larger of the two. Jimmy was slight of build, but not as small as Percy. Thankfully, it was he, not Joey, who was circling the front of the car. He'd almost reached Percy when the driver-side door opened, also, and Joey got out, towering over Jimmy. Through the open car door, Percy could see a baseball bat lying across the front seat. That didn't bode well.

"I've been trying to call you two."

Joey stepped in front of him. "Liar," he said.

"Hey, I was going to…"

A second later, Jimmy's hands closed around Percy's throat. Breath was cut off. Then he felt his back hit the side of the car as Jimmy slammed him against it. Pain reverberated through his entire body, and his insides shook like jelly. "I know I owe Big Frank," Percy gasped as the fingers on his neck loosened.

"It's good you're aware of that fact," Joey said, his voice gravelly. "That means you're going to do what we say or else."

"Do?" What were they talking about? Percy's mind raced, and otherwise, he was filled with self-loathing. Just moments before, he'd been so sure that finding Ellie meant his luck was about to change. "I know I owe Big Frank," he repeated. "But I'm not gambling anymore. I haven't placed a bet since…"

Since he'd found out Ellie was coming into his life. Yes, the call about the poll she'd conducted had been that significant. Not only because Ellie was a gorgeous catch, but because it meant the tide had finally turned for Percy. It was as if the hand of God, himself, had come into Percy's life to rescue him, and all Percy had to do was make good on what he'd been given.

Since that day, the very same day Helen had asked him for a date to the movies, Percy hadn't been to the track once. Horses had been his weakness, but after the call, he'd taken the betting sheets he'd so feared Helen would find and destroyed them. Ever since she'd come on board as his assistant, he'd done nothing but worry about her discovering his secret life. She'd had such an impeccable resume, and he respected her so much….

"I know I still owe Big Frank some money," he began

again. "And you know I work as an accountant. You know I'm good for what I owe, but it'll take a few weeks, a couple more paychecks. I can get Big Frank half on Friday, the other half two Fridays down the road. Okay, guys?"

The fingers wrapped around his neck once more and tightened until Percy was sure he'd cease to be able to breathe. "Okay?" he gasped once more.

"No, it's not okay," Joey said.

"No, you worthless piece of garbage, it's not. But you got lucky this time around. Big Frank is going to show his mercy."

Relief flooded Percy. "He is?"

"Only if you do something for him," Joey assured him. "Nothing's for free."

"What?" What on earth could Percy do for a man like Big Frank?

"Get in the car and find out," muttered Jimmy, releasing his hold on Percy's neck, but only long enough to grasp his upper arm and steer him toward the car's back door. As soon as Joey opened it, the two men pushed Percy inside. The door slammed, then Joey and Jimmy got back inside the vehicle.

There was no use making a run for it, Percy decided. Both men were faster than he. And anyway, he deserved what he got. He'd been a fool to get involved in betting on horses. He'd just discovered the track a couple years ago, and at first, had only gambled for casual fun.

But then, about a year ago, he'd hit a tough patch. Nothing seemed to be going right. Work was lousy, and his folks had both fallen ill. They were fine now, but he'd run himself ragged between caretaking duties and the office.

During that time, the gambling had started to feel less like a hobby and more like a compulsion. He'd grab an hour and go to the track, where he could really let go. When he had money on a horse, all his problems would seem to vanish.

Excitement coursed through his veins as the sleek animals breezed toward the home stretch. All around him, crowds cheered and shouted. Then there was nothing but the fast pounding of hooves and the feeling that this time he, Percy Anders, might be a real winner.

He never was.

Now he waited, terror coiling through his veins as he stared toward the front seat. "Look," he told them. "I said I'd pay you guys. Big Frank will get his money. You know I'm good for it."

One of Joey's beefy fists reached around the headrest to grab ahold of Percy. Joey's eyes settled on Percy, containing absolutely no compassion, as if Percy were a bug. "Like we're saying, Big Frank has a job for you."

Percy's eyes widened. "Me?"

"Yeah, you," said Jimmy.

"What does he want me to do?"

Joey surveyed Percy, then said, "Listen up, because it's real important. And it's got to do with your little lady friend, Ellie Lee."

"I could never hurt Ellie," Percy murmured.

Joey glared at him. "You'll do whatever we tell you to do."

5

THE RINGING PHONE startled Ellie and she yelped, then she pressed a hand over her heart to still its wild beating. She'd been so lost in thought, she had no idea how long she'd been leaning against the door. Minutes could have passed or hours.

"Drats," she muttered. Spending the evening with Percy had aroused countless unwanted recollections of Robby. Unwittingly, due to his sheer undesirability, the other man had left her aching for things she knew she'd never experience again—Robby's big, warm hands slowly gliding over her body, his hot, hungry mouth bathing her bare skin in kisses, his strangled cries as he buried himself deep inside her, making her moan with the unbelievable pleasure. Now the months she'd spent in Robby's bed seemed like a crazy dream she'd only imagined.

Shaking her head to clear it of confusion, she needed to get moving. Yes, she needed to get changed and sleep, she thought, blowing out a sigh. She had a big day tomorrow, and before she knew it, it would be morning and Angelina would be showing up for work.

Absently, she dug into her shoulder bag, searching for the phone. At first, she'd assumed it was her landline, but it was the cell. When she found it, she glanced down at the screen, but she didn't recognize the number.

"Oh, no," she moaned. Ten to one, it was Percy calling to say good-night. Maybe she shouldn't answer, she decided, but that was rude. Dreading the conversation, she pressed the talk button and raised the phone to her ear.

Feeling sure she knew what was coming, she braced herself and tried to sound polite. "Hello?"

There was a long pause during which she heard heavy breathing. Her heart hammered. Maybe Percy really was a stalker or psycho. But no, she thought, schooling herself not to let her mind run away, he was just nerdy. "Uh…Percy?"

Still, no answer.

She tried once more. "Percy?"

"No. This isn't Percy."

"Robby?" She bit back a gasp of surprise. Why was he calling her? A stab of fear hit her. In a flash, she remembered the call, months ago, when it was assumed J. D. Johnson had died in the explosion on his boat, *The Alabama.* Robby was the one who'd informed Susannah. Had something happened to one of her family members?

"Daddy?" she managed to ask, her mind racing. Her father was getting on in years. For a split second, she kicked herself for treating him so meanly. Had his high blood pressure become more of a problem? Was she to blame?

"No," Robby said quickly. "Nothing like that. Everybody is fine."

Relief flooded her and she sighed, then she hoped he hadn't noticed. No, she'd prefer that Robby not guess how much she'd been thinking about Banner. A burst of anger exploded, then wended through her veins, since the call was so unexpected. "Well, if everybody is okay, why did you scare me like this?"

"I didn't think I'd scare you, Ellie. I was just calling you."

"Of course you scared me!"

"Why?"

He was being intentionally obtuse. "Because you called out of the blue!"

"Sorry."

Silently, she kicked herself for taking the call. "Sorry's not good enough."

"I didn't call to fight."

"Then why did you call?" Months had gone by during which she'd never heard a peep. Oh, maybe she'd hoped he'd call and apologize or try to get her back. She glanced at the clock. "And it's the middle of the night."

"It's ten."

"My bedtime."

"You don't need to remind me."

An uncomfortable silence followed. Certainly, she hadn't wanted to recall how well Robby knew her intimate habits. Just to spite him, she assured him, "I go to bed later now. At midnight. Sometimes even later than that. In fact, I'm often still awake at one. This is the city that never sleeps."

He offered a soft male grunt of frustration. "In that case, why did you yell at me for keeping you up? You're not making sense, Ellie."

"I didn't yell at you."

He sighed. "This is not going well," he muttered.

"Who are you talking to?" she demanded. "Daddy?"

"No!" he exploded.

"Oh, you called me just to talk to yourself?" Her voice sharpened. "Where are you, anyway?" He sounded so close he could have been on the other side of the door. "And why are you calling me?"

"I want to make an appointment to talk to you."

"We're talking now."

"I mean in person."

"About?"

Another long pause ensued, then he said, "Business. It's strictly business, Ellie."

"Business," she fumed, as if that said it all.

Now he grunted again, as if to say she was impossible. "Would you rather it was personal?"

Was it her imagination or had he sounded hopeful? "Of course not."

"Good. Because like I said, it is business, strictly business."

And her surge of anger pumped through her veins, and she wasn't sure why. "Look, Robby, I know we're in the same industry, and it's a small world. No doubt, we'll have to speak from time to time—" Abruptly stopping herself, she wondered why they would have to cross paths after all, then she plunged on. "But tonight isn't the best time."

"I'm getting that impression."

Glancing around, she took in the expensive furnishings. The carpet was new, the black lacquered desk gleaming, graced with a sterling vase brimming with gorgeous red tulips. The fireplace in the room didn't work, but it was decorative, as was the two-by-four Asian rug in front of the hearth. Her attention settled on the file cabinets in the corner, then a bank of computer equipment against the far wall. She'd done well for herself, dammit. Nevertheless, just hearing Robby's voice made her feel about the size of an ant. Deep down, it was as if he rejected her, not the other way around. And he must have known how she'd respond to his betrayal.

She drew a steadying breath. Oh, she'd lost her mind over the man, however briefly. Maybe throughout most of her life, she admitted. But that was before she'd actually slept with him. As a girl, she'd been drawn in by his rough-and-tumble past and bad-boy aura. He'd been gorgeous to look at, and not in her league by virtue of age and breeding. Later, he'd become a colleague, but never a friend.

No, she and Robby Robriquet could never be buddies. There had always been too much raw, sexual male-female tension between them. In each encounter, the very air had seemed to come alive and bristle. Just hearing his voice, she felt edgy, nervous and flinty in a way she found hard to tolerate. As if a match might suddenly strike and she'd literally burn to a crisp.

Inevitably, they'd wound up in bed. It had been pure bliss, at first, everything she'd ever dreamed. Thinking of him still made her shudder all over. She could hear his voice in her ears, taste his flesh in her mouth, feel his skin beneath her hands. Yes, she'd sleep with him again. She wouldn't be able to help herself. But that's all it could ever be….

Just sex. Getting their ya-yas out because they were horny. It would mean nothing. She'd never be so foolish as to dream of anything more. Weddings were for people like Angelina and Antonio, who were uncomplicated. But she and Robby….

"Are you still there, Ellie?"

"Yeah," she replied, glad her voice didn't betray the myriad emotions coursing through her. "Only taking a minute to check my blood pressure."

"Mad because I called?"

"Oh, no," she chided. "It was exactly what I needed to top off my evening. Better than any nightcap."

"You can still have one of those," he said. "To take the edge off."

"Edge?"

"You do sound pissed." He was starting to sound testy, himself, since this conversation seemed to be going nowhere. Not that his tone did anything to undercut the effect his voice had on her. It was low and throaty, gravelly and undeniably male. Every time she heard it, she felt as if she'd just put a hand on his hard, hairy chest; yes, she'd settled her long fingers right between his luscious pectorals, and the vibrations reverberated through their tips, right to her soul. That sweet drawl made memories of Mississippi wash over her, too, and she missed her folks, J.D. and Susannah, not to mention the Night Rider and Delia's Diner. She felt a strong pull at her heart, a tug she was powerless to deny, and all she wanted was for him to come get her and take her home.

She hated Robby for that, as well. Why, if it wasn't for him, she'd be in her own beloved, two-bedroom house, the one that was going to the weeds. No doubt, her mother had done as asked, and hired someone to clean the place weekly and landscape the yard. Still, those were jobs Ellie usually enjoyed herself. And it was her house!

Pulling herself together, she said, "Now, why do you want to see me?"

"Strictly business, like I said."

"Can you be more specific?"

"Not until I see you."

"You want to come to New York?"

"Yeah."

"I don't know how I feel about that, Robby. We don't have anything to discuss."

"I think we do."

"Let me think about it."

"Until when?"

"A few days."

"Why not now?"

"I have a lot going on."

"Like what?"

God, he was grilling her, and she was hardly in the mood. It had been a strange, disappointing night. "Just things."

"What things?"

"Things, Robby!"

"I need an answer."

"I don't remember you being quite this dictatorial."

During the pause, she could hear his breath. Finally, he murmured in a throaty, sexy voice, "I'm nicer when I'm sharing a bed with a woman."

"Well, then, you should go find a woman."

"I mean you."

"You're supposed to be nice no matter what."

"So you're not going to acknowledge what I just said?"

For a second, she couldn't get words past her tongue. She felt as if his arms had just wrapped tightly around her chest and squeezed. "No. And like I said, you're supposed to be nice—"

"All the time? I don't live in the land of shoulda, coulda, woulda."

So he wasn't going to apologize for what had transpired months ago. Another silence fell. Against her will, she wanted to ask him how things were going. Had her activities put a dent in Lee Polls' business? Or were they doing okay? She was a competitor, yes, but she cared about Lee Polls, too. She wondered how her mom was fairing, as well, not to mention her dad. Had he managed to stay out of the office? And was his retirement going well?

What about Sheriff Kemp and Delia from the diner? Were they still dating? And another thought niggled. She'd almost forgotten, she realized with horror. Wasn't Robby's father, Charlie, getting out of jail? She searched her mind, but couldn't recall his exact release date. Her father would know, of course. He remembered everything, but Ellie couldn't call him.

The event wasn't exactly something Robby liked to talk about. Oh, she'd probed him countless times, but he never wanted to discuss feelings about his father. *And you threw the man up in his face,* a voice nagged. Heat warmed her cheeks at the recollection. Had she really compared Robby to Charlie? The two were polar opposites. Everybody in Banner knew that. And while she'd been furious, it was no excuse. Should she apologize now? Or wait for another time? Would there be another time?

Or maybe she shouldn't apologize. The morning she'd left Robby, she'd wanted to hurt him as much as humanly possible, but clearly she hadn't succeeded, since he was calling her.

"No, you don't live in shoulda, coulda, woulda," she finally agreed, blowing out a long breath.

He was a realist. A doer. He never looked back. His father had been pure scum, and Robby had tolerated his behavior for years. When Charlie crossed the ultimate line, however, Robby had cut him loose without a backward glance. Maybe he felt the same about her. He hadn't even mentioned the newspaper article, although he must have seen it.

"It's strictly business, Ellie," he said again.

"Why don't you call me in the morning." She was unsure if she was suggesting it because she wanted to see Robby, or because she was curious about what he had up his sleeve. "Whatever this pertains to…did Daddy put you up to it?"

The pause was a fraction too long, long enough that she knew she'd called it right. She scarcely wanted to examine the confused feelings that assaulted her now, mostly disappointment, sadness and loneliness all combined, then another prickle of pure pique. Of course Robby hadn't called her of his own volition. Daddy Eddie had made him, which meant this truly was business.

And when it came to business, Ellie trusted her father even less than her ex-lover. "Robby?"

"True…Daddy Eddie did suggest I pay you a visit," Robby admitted.

"Then, I'll get back to you," she muttered. "When it suits me."

With that, she pressed the phone's off button. The second she'd done so, she felt strangely forlorn. Now Robby would guess at her true feelings, however complex they might be. Why hadn't she been cooler, more nonchalant? She could have made an appointment with him, just as he'd requested, as if the meeting meant absolutely nothing to her.

And then she could have seen him again. Sighing, she stared toward the foldout couch in the other room. Definitely, it looked inviting. She still had to take off her makeup, though, and since she was wearing high heels, her feet were killing her. Maybe sleep would help. Right about now, it was pretty clear nothing could redeem this day. Placing the cell into her purse again, she moved to push herself off the door. Just as she did so, a knock sounded from the other side.

Frowning, she turned. The lobby door shut after Percy had gone; she'd checked and it locked automatically. "Oh, it must be Ms. Kilpatrick," she whispered. The lonely widow in the apartment directly above Ellie often dropped by, usually with some homemade baked goods. Obviously, she could hear Ellie come and go because she usually arrived moments after Ellie came home. It was as if Ms. Kilpatrick was waiting.

Despite being stuffed to the gills from a long dinner at Oh, Susannah's, Ellie recalled a particularly tasty blueberry pie Ms. Kilpatrick had once brought, and her stomach rumbled. She wasn't proud of it, but after the conversation with Robby, she'd welcome any form of comfort food. Feeling relieved at the prospect of the elderly woman's friendly face after such a stressful evening, Ellie opened the door wide.

Her hand froze around the doorknob so tightly that she was sure no human force could pry it away. Her smile froze, too, and she felt like a statue in a town square, immobile and rooted to the spot. Except she wasn't made of granite, at least not judging by the rapid beat of her heart.

Whatever the real reason for his visit, Robby Robriquet sure hadn't dressed for business. She was used to seeing him in suits, but tonight he was clad in a brown sports coat worn over a Western-style plaid shirt and well-washed jeans. An old army duffel was slung over his shoulder, and since she recognized it as one in which he'd carried clothes when he'd visited her home, it was if he'd come to spend the night with her.

Which he hadn't, she reminded herself firmly. Not that she didn't want him. What woman wouldn't? He looked older, somehow, but that was crazy, since she'd seen him only months ago when she'd visited Banner. She'd glimpsed her dad then, too, not that they'd spoken at length. Only her mother had cornered Ellie and insisted on a heart-to-heart, begging Ellie to come home.

"You shouldn't be in a city all by yourself," her mother had said.

"I'm fine," Ellie had assured her.

But was she? Oh, she was doing well business-wise, but… Her eyes drifted to Robby. He'd lost weight and looked a little gaunt, but if the truth be told, it only made him look sexier than ever, lending his face a craggy, Western aura. All he was missing was a Stetson hat, such as the one J. D. Johnson always wore. Robby wasn't a particularly large man, although his height exceeded her five foot seven inches. Otherwise, he was tough and stocky, all ridges and bunched-up rock-hard muscles. Lying against him felt like lying against granite, and she'd loved it. No man had ever made her feel so soft and feminine.

"I thought you were in Banner," she blurted.

His eyes were squinting, the blue irises lost to the shadows of the hallway, giving nothing away. When he spoke, his voice was unnervingly casual, provocatively matter-of-fact. His tone bespoke the attitude of a man who was studying his nails, or chewing lazily on a blade of grass. Something that only served to pronounce his sugary Mississippi drawl, making homesickness surge inside her once more.

Stepping forward, he leaned against the door frame, so she couldn't exactly shut the door. "Did I fail to mention I was in town?"

She laid her own drawl on just as thick for his benefit. "Yes, I believe you did leave that pertinent fact out of our conversation."

"Then it's a good thing I'm here to correct myself," he returned, his eyes drifting slowly over her, the heat in his gaze reminding her that she was wearing a gold silk shawl draped over a slinky black cocktail dress with capped sleeves. She was powerless not to notice the sharp intake of breath when his eyes hit the hem of the dress, then traveled down the black stockings to her spike heels. "You know my work habits better than anyone, so you know I hate oversights."

"You're a stickler for details," she agreed cautiously.

"And tonight I see you didn't miss a trick."

She knew damn well he was talking about her outfit, guessing she'd been on a date. "This close to Halloween a lot of people are thinking about tricks."

His eyes flicked over her once more, lingering at the plunging neckline of the dress, studying the cleavage. His voice turned husky. "Or treats."

"Or turning into pumpkins at midnight."

His gaze had started traveling again, this time roving over her breasts, making her aware that she was exposed. Inadvertently, she sucked in a quick, audible breath, making her chest rise, as if for his perusal. Worse, her nipples beaded almost painfully beneath the fabric, and she had to fight the urge to pull the shawl more tightly around her shoulders. Somehow, she managed not to do so. Definitely, she didn't want him guessing that his unexpected appearance on her doorstep had sent her into a tizzy.

"You're still a witch," he said in an almost whisper.

"It's you who was the demon."

He didn't deny it. "Are you going to invite me in?"

"Thought you wanted to make an appointment."

"I did."

"Fine. My office doesn't open until tomorrow. You'll need to talk to my assistant."

"I'd rather talk to you." His attention had settled on her breasts once more, making a hot flush infuse her limbs. It tingled to her toes and fizzled.

"So I take it the matter is pressing?" It must be, for him to fly all the way to New York, but from the man's glazed expression, Ellie felt pretty sure he didn't have business on the brain.

"Very." His gaze found hers now, and it came as a shock to her system. She'd forgotten how intently Robby could look at her, as if she were the only woman in the world. "Can I come…"

His voice trailed off and the last word he'd spoken hung in the air, the sexual connotation crystal clear. He could, indeed. In fact, he had many times, holding her in his arms. "Come in?" she finished for him.

"Right."

Her feet seemed to move of their own accord, and she stepped back a pace, now wondering if he'd even bothered to book a room somewhere. "Seeing as you've come such a long way…"

"I appreciate your hospitality, ma'am," he drawled. And in the next moment, he swept inside, shutting the door behind him. After that, they were truly alone, with no possibility of intrusion from Ellie's prying neighbors. Ellie could only stare at her visitor. Had Robby Robriquet really just called, then breezed into her life again? And why now, when he'd had months to come calling? Whatever the case, she was about to get her answers.

6

As soon as the door closed, Robby realized he'd made a mistake. Ellie looked too hot and smelled too damn good. Sugar and spice and everything nice entered his nostrils, making them flare, her scent alone enough to bring him to his knees. Despite his best intentions, he wasn't going to be able to keep his hands off her even though he knew he should.

Still, wasn't sex with her what he'd really come for? His senses heightening, he told himself he'd better turn around and go back to Banner. That was the smart thing to do. If they did kiss and make up, she'd only get mad about something else down the road, then leave him again. Despite how he craved her touch, Robby had experienced enough instability while growing up with his old man. He liked to know where he stood. Besides, Ellie had had the nerve to compare him to Charlie, which was unforgivable.

Unfortunately, he was male, and she was wearing the sexiest dress he'd ever seen, so he couldn't help but stare. The nearly black hair he'd run his hands through countless times had been tamed into a perfect bob that grazed her chin. It had just a touch of red, making him wonder if she'd used some sort of dye or rinse, but then he noticed the touchable strands were merely affected by the light.

She'd turned off the overhead illumination and flicked on a table lamp, so the glow was doing wonders for the rest of her—making her peaches-and-cream skin glow, her swollen, pink-painted lips glisten, her gossamer golden shawl shine like a beacon. His heart stuttered as he took in the swaths of black fabric loosely cupping her breasts, just the way his hands itched to do. There seemed to be a catch at the collar of the dress, one he could unhook with a quick gesture that would make the bodice fall to her waist. Or maybe that was just wishful thinking.

Determined not to let his eyes linger too long, he tried, but failed, to glance away. A pang of longing claimed his groin then, and his jeans felt so tight he almost groaned out loud.

Damn, she'd never dressed like this for him. Usually, he saw her in perfunctory business suits, not that she didn't look great in them. Still…this dress was hot, at least what he could see peeking out from beneath the shawl, and he wanted her. Now. Right here. When his gaze stopped on the hem of the cocktail sheath where it skimmed her knees, every male cell of his body felt charged with electricity. He was sure hoping the black stockings she wore were made of raw silk and that they had a sexy seam in back.

Wow. His lips parted, so he could tell her to turn around and let him look, but then he thought the better of saying anything. Nevertheless, every time he focused on her, it got harder to remember they were supposed to be fighting. So what if she'd compared him to his old man? Okay, just a moment ago, that had seemed unforgivable, but now…

Have a heart, he pleaded silently. If he softened toward her, could she forget his betrayal? Making up with her wouldn't change a thing, anyway. Daddy Eddie was set in his ways, and at Lee Polls, he'd never replace Robby with his daughter. Once he'd made decisions, he stuck to them.

Robby sighed once more, wondering what to do about his undeniable lust for Ellie. Her eyes captured his attention, the gaze cool and confident. It was distant, too, difficult to read, and a little judgmental, almost contemptuous. But what the hell had he done wrong? Could he help it if her dad had promoted him, not her?

And who was Percy Anders, really? Her dream man, no doubt, Robby thought, bristling with displeasure when he thought of the article about her gimmick in the newspaper. Yeah, right. Robby had stood on a street corner, not an hour ago, staring through the window of Oh, Susannah's, watching Ellie flirt with the man, and even now it made his temper spike. The guy had seemed like a total weasel. Robby could take him down with one arm tied behind his back. Yet the man and Ellie had seemed to be enjoying themselves.

Worse, he'd waited on the sidewalk while Percy said good-night, and the guy had stayed inside the vestibule longer than Robby would have liked. Surely, Ellie hadn't actually kissed the guy, had she? Hell, maybe it was a real relationship, not just a gimmick. Definitely, Ellie had conducted a genuine poll. Yesterday, Robby had confirmed that much. But how could such a dud be the best mate for Ellie?

Incredulous annoyance swept over him. Well, appearance wasn't everything. Maybe the man possessed intriguing knowledge, or excessive compassion, or interesting hobbies— all things women liked. Although Percy Anders sure as hell didn't look like a hunter or a fisherman.

Robby had called the newspaper on the sly, and a man named Derrick Mills, who'd promised not to tell Ellie about the call, had reported that Percy was an accountant. At least, on some level, Percy would be able to talk shop with Ellie, Robby considered, trying to be charitable.

So what, so could Robby! Pure fury coursed through him. It hardly helped his mood that Charlie was out of jail now, and Robby had nearly run into him a couple of times. Yet another reason for getting the hell out of Dodge. Damn the man for showing his face at Delia's Diner, Robby fumed. Then he got angry all over again, since Delia had the nerve to hire his father to wash dishes in the diner. Why was the fool woman giving a loser like Charlie a second chance?

More like a millionth chance, Robby amended, thinking of Charlie's many transgressions over the years. Apparently, his old man was renting a room at Hodge's Motor Lodge and paying by the month. The only saving grace was that he hadn't visited the Night Rider, which would have been a violation of his parole.

It was a sad day when the only safe haven for Robby was the local pub. Slipping the duffel off his shoulder, he let it slide to the floor near the door. Quickly, he glanced around; once he'd shrugged off thoughts about his father, he sought Ellie again, the temptation too great. "Are you going to offer me a drink or should I have brought my own bottle?"

"A whole bottle? Does that mean you're staying a while?"

As long as you'll let me, he thought, eyeing the dress. "Just for a drink."

She merely surveyed him, then she raised an eyebrow and said, "What? Let me guess. They ran out of whiskey in Banner, Mississippi?"

As if. Clancy O'Dell's family had gotten their start during prohibition. Hell would freeze over before the Night Rider would run out of booze, but if Ellie wanted to spar, Robby could play the game. "Didn't Clancy call to tell you the well dried up?"

She shook her head.

He offered a nonchalant shrug. "That's what you get when you leave town without a forwarding address."

"And what's that?"

"Cut out of the loop."

"So Clancy closed shop?"

Of course not and she knew it. "Hardly."

"It would be a pity. That bar's been around almost as long as Lee Polls," she added before he could respond. "A truly sad story… I mean, if it did close."

Not as sad as their own romance. "Anyway, all's not lost," Robby assured her. "'Cause, assuming their tap really had run dry, I seem to have landed at Ellie's bar."

She smirked at that. "Lucky me."

"It's your day, darlin'."

Her alluring bee-stung lips pouted more than usual, if it could be imagined, making his heart beat double time. God, he was hungry for that mouth. He wanted to devour, to plunder. The woman damn well knew the effect she had on him, too.

Without moving a muscle, he could feel his arms wrapping around her, her lips crushing beneath his. In a flash, his mouth would cover hers entirely, he thought, then her soft, warm tongue would come out to play, tussling and struggling against his as if they were locked in a mortal battle in which only one of them would survive. Then he'd take off her dress…

And all the while, they'd be getting turned on, until they were hot enough to scorch an iron. In his mind's eye, he could see her tilting back her head to give him better access, exposing the long, slender column of her neck to the ministrations of his mouth as he ripped off her dress and dragged her to the floor.

Didn't she know they belonged together? Oh, he wasn't good enough for her. They'd both always known that. She was well-bred, if aggressive for a female. But he'd always liked that about her. He, too, could act like an animal. In fact, she brought it out in him, making him feel dangerous, almost predatory at times, purely male.

Every time he looked at her, something dangerously magical and darkly unforgettable began flowing through his veins.

Then sparks flew. Lights flickered as if due to some short-circuiting current and molecules danced in the air.

"Whiskey?" she finally asked.

Her voice drew him from the reverie. Whiskey was what he usually drank, but now he wanted to play the contrarian, if only to shock her by asking for something else. Call him slightly sadistic, but he wanted her to think he'd changed and that she didn't even know him anymore. It would throw her off-kilter and erode the damnable confidence in her eyes. If the truth be told, her attitude was starting to drive him a little crazy.

He wasn't sure what he'd expected. Certainly not tears of joy, or for her to fling herself into his arms and beg him to forgive her for walking out on him. He sighed. Whatever the case, he did enjoy whiskey and, knowing Ellie, the only other alcoholic beverage she'd have in the apartment would be wine. That and milk, which would hardly provide worthwhile stimulation. "Straight up," he told her. "Ice if you can manage it."

"Manage it? Why, I thought coldness was my specialty."

He'd never said that, and it was time to let her know she was playing with fire. "Heat," he returned without missing a beat, his voice low. "Not cold. You know I never said that about you, Ellie."

"Maybe not, but you thought it."

She could be calculating, yes, but not cold. "Sheer projection on your part," he remarked. "And you never were much of a mind reader."

"No?"

Yes, he amended, at least when it came to her gauging how to touch and kiss him. He shook his head. "No."

She shrugged as if to say it didn't matter either way. "Well, I've been up north so long," she drawled, "that I'm not sure I can remember any of the fine female arts."

"Such as serving a man a whiskey?"

She tilted her head as if to get a better look at him. "You could get it yourself."

"I don't know where you keep your liquor," he countered.

She heaved a sigh, one so exaggerated that he could tell her exasperation wasn't at all genuine. In fact, the feigned pique was a little flirtatious, but Robby wasn't going to take it as a hint.

She said, "Then I suppose I could get it for you."

"All's not lost. You can fix yourself one, too."

"Oh, no," she chided with a soft chuckle, as if to make clear that she'd never trust his motives. He didn't blame her. It had been quite a while since the two had shared a drink without it leading to them also sharing a bed.

"No?"

"I'd like to keep my wits about me during your visit," she continued, turning to head for the kitchen. "Your brief visit," she emphasized.

When he saw the back of her legs, he wasn't sure he could vouch for that time frame. Bands seemed to circle around his chest, stealing his breath. Her legs were truly breathtaking, he thought, like masterpieces of fine art—long, gently curved and gorgeous. That her stockings did, in fact, have dark seams was enough to make his already rising testosterone levels shoot into the stratosphere.

"Don't mind me," he called after her, as she vanished into the kitchen. "Feel free to pour yourself something strong, since I don't plan on putting any moves on you." It wasn't strictly true, but he felt compelled to say it, anyway.

"Then you must have changed a lot, Robby," she called.

"I was left with no choice," he returned, raising his voice so she could hear. "You know how it is. Overworked and underpaid." That wasn't true, either. Daddy Eddie compensated generously.

"Boo hoo. The next thing you know you'll be telling me your girlfriend left you, too."

"And you know how men tend to get when that happens," he quipped. "Footloose and fancy-free."

"Why, of course," she shot back in a heartbeat. "I'm surprised you could find the time to drop by so unexpectedly."

"What can I say? A plane happened to be right in front of me."

"Happens to me all the time."

A silence fell, then suddenly she called, "So you're working double time without me?"

The damnable woman actually sounded pleased. "Only because Lee Polls is considering myriad future directions."

She let that pass. "A shot or an old-fashioned glass?"

Actually, after looking at Ellie, a highball glass was more what he had in mind. Only that much booze could numb his nerve endings, since they wouldn't stop tingling. "Your choice."

"If you'll trust me."

He barely heard. He was too busy looking around the room, gathering whatever information he could. Clearly she'd been running the business on a shoestring. Ellie would, he thought now. She was smart and thrifty. At Lee Polls, she'd always gone over the books, finding ways to cut costs.

Here, she'd done a great job. The living room had been transformed into an attractive office. His gut tightened when he glanced into one of the rooms beyond where a foldout couch was open, made up with what looked like fresh sheets.

Unable not to visualize his own king-size bed, and then Ellie's serviceable queen, he sighed. God, how he missed leaning against her hopelessly feminine white cane headboard, with the delicate eyelet quilt drawn up to their necks. Both beds beat the hell out of what she was sleeping on now he thought, once more studying the foldout, which, despite the sheets, looked small and uncomfortable.

Reentering the room, she caught his gaze, then tried to pretend she hadn't. "One whiskey," she said. "Coming up."

"Thanks."

His eyes trailed once more over her figure—from touchable breasts that called out for his hands, to the rolling, swaying hips, the mile-long legs, the slender, sloping shape of sexy black shoes that hugged her feet.

"So you changed your mind," he said, glancing at the two glasses as she stepped lightly in front of him and handed him one. As he took the whiskey, their fingertips brushed and it affected his system like a shot of fire. Immediately, he sipped the booze, and it warmed his mouth, then beat a trail of heat right down to his belly. If he hadn't been staring at Ellie, he might have mistakenly believed the warmth pooling in his groin was the drink, but as his eyes dipped into cleavage once more, he knew that would be a lie. "Thanks," he murmured.

"Sure," she said, whirling away a bit too quickly, as if reading his mind. She headed for a wing chair, one of two that banked the fireplace, opposite the main desk, and seated herself. It was classic Ellie. Elegant, cool, sophisticated. Beyond him. When she crossed her legs, it only served to make the hem of her dress rise, showing him more thigh than he thought he could handle.

Blowing out a surreptitious breath, he tried to steady his nerves with another shot of whiskey. Damn, it tasted good, sliding slowly down his throat, burning another pathway to his belly. Only her mouth could have tasted hotter. His eyes never left hers as she took a slow sip. He expected her to wince, but she didn't, just extended a long, graceful arm and set the glass on a small, two-tiered table beside her.

"I thought you hated whiskey," he said. She usually went for the girly drinks, such as Baileys Irish Cream or White Russians. Maybe a glass of wine.

"It's all I have in the house," she said simply.

Somehow, he didn't believe her. Something in her voice made him decide it was his presence that had called for the heavy stuff. He didn't know what to say after that, and otherwise, he suddenly wished the room wasn't so quiet. Nor could he suggest she turn on a TV, since he didn't see one.

As if reading his mind, she reached beside her and leaned. Only then did he realize the table had a small compact CD player rested on the second tier, tucked out of sight. Classical piano music filled the room. No doubt what she used during regular office hours.

"No Garth Brooks?"

"I've got some of J.D.'s stuff," she said. "Susannah brought them last time she visited. Would you rather...?"

"No," he said quickly, shaking his head, hardly wanting her to think he'd like to listen to his buddy croon love songs. "Susannah was here just a couple weeks ago, right?" he asked, already knowing the answer, scarcely able to believe he was trying to make small talk. It felt artificial. The bed was a few feet away—a foldout couch, anyway—and that was where they should get down to business. Yes, whatever matters be broached, he and Ellie would better discuss them in bed.

She nodded. "Susannah's been coming in a lot, more than she really needs, since her restaurant's so successful. But I'm glad to see her."

Was it his imagination, or had Ellie's voice carried wistfulness? Was she homesick? At nothing more than the thought, he had to fight not to cross the room and gather her into his arms. "She said you don't have much time to visit when she comes," he said. "That you're staying busy."

Whatever passed in Ellie's eyes was hard to read—curiosity, dread, frustration. Possibly she felt betrayed that he and Susannah had been talking about her. "What else?"

"Did she say?" He shook his head, sampling another si

of whiskey. "Not much. She said her manager is excellent, and the cooks and waitstaff love Oh, Susannah's and treat the restaurant like a second home."

"She's still got the original employees with which she started," Ellie added. "And it's true. They're like family."

Ellie would notice that, since she'd grown up in the atmosphere of a family business. Changing the subject, she said, "Aren't you going to sit?"

The longer he looked at those mouthwatering legs, encased in black stockings, the more difficult it was to recall the real reason for his visit. "Sure," he said, leaning, zipping open the duffel and pulling out a file folder. "I brought some papers for you to look at, if you don't mind."

Her shoulders straightened and she shifted her weight in the wing chair, correcting her posture. "Papers?"

Strolling toward her, he lithely dropped the folder into her lap, then he turned and seated himself opposite her, in the identical wing chair. He was close enough that her scent wafted to his nostrils once more, making them flare. She was wearing a new perfume, one he'd never smelled before, and it was pungent, bursting with complexity. Subtle and smooth, it bespoke fruit spices and warm cream.

It was the wrong time to feel another rush of arousal, but the room felt too quiet again, although music was playing. Too warm, too, although, in reality, the temperature was just right. Ellie had already set aside her drink and opened the folder. "What's this?"

"It should be self-explanatory."

He looked on as she shuffled pages for a few silent moments, her eyes narrowing, her sexy lips pursing. He couldn't tell if she was getting angry or merely concentrating.

Without looking up, she murmured, "You want to buy Future Trends?"

"I think you'll see it's a firm offer."

"What makes you think I'll sell?"

"Because it's a good deal."

"But I just started my company, and it's doing well," she said, glancing at him before studying the papers again. "In fact, I'm running one of the more interesting promotional campaigns in the history of the polling business."

Obviously she was referring to the gimmick with Percy Anders. He didn't think it was much of a campaign, but he let that slide. "I get that. I…" He wasn't about to tell her that he'd called Derrick Mills, the reporter who'd first covered the story. "I read the article in the newspaper."

"So already you're aware you're offering far too little money for my start-up?"

"Maybe," he conceded, taking another sip of whiskey, and feeling encouraged she was even considering the deal. Hell, he'd expected her to toss the folder right back into his face. "And as you know, we can negotiate."

"Uh-huh," she prompted. "And…"

"As you see," he continued, "Lee Polls can sell some holdings in order to make the purchase. It's a solid offer, Ellie. With a little tinkering, you'll wind up with more from the offer than you'll get elsewhere."

"What makes you think I was thinking about selling?"

"Because if you haven't yet, you will. Besides, it's in the interest of both companies in the long run. We can't compete. While you're on top now, I suspect that will turn around in another year when some of Lee's steadier, longer-term, biannual clients start drifting back. You know as well as I do that if you'd started your company a year from now, you wouldn't be able to steal as many clients."

"I didn't steal."

Of course she had. "Whatever."

She relaxed in her chair and surveyed him. She really was considering the deal. If the truth be told, that was the last thing he'd expected. He'd thought this was a long shot.

She shrugged. "Why should I have pity on Lee Polls?"

"Pity?"

"Well, if both companies stand to lose in the long run, why shouldn't I buy you out, instead?"

"Because you started Future Trends to get back at your father and me," he said, speaking matter-of-factly. "You've done it, too. You've proven you can shift the whole industry your way. Simultaneously, you've set up a satellite office in a major hub, which we can jointly use to double our business. And by now, I figure you're getting hungry again."

"For?"

"You could run this office while working to expand our work in Florida."

She stared at him. "Florida?"

"I was thinking about Miami." Pausing, he drained the last of the whiskey, then shook the glass for good measure, listening to the ice jingle. "You've taken some of our top clients. But more important, you've brought a new class of clients on board, mostly because you've sought to break into other industries."

"True. You and Daddy Eddie rely on local and national elections, but I've started bringing in more corporate clients. Next, I intend to make inroads into governmental contracts. You know that's where the big money is."

He nodded. "Exactly my point. So maybe we nix Florida and move you to D.C. If that's the direction you want to go."

"You'd want to keep me on?"

"More than that. You'd be a director."

"Sort of a…"

"Co-president. Along with me. We could do it together,

Ellie." He paused. "We don't need to make it personal. You wouldn't have to return to Banner…not if you don't want. We could turn Lee Polls into a much larger business, with offices in several cities. Your father will love it. He's never wanted to lose the Banner location, of course, but he's talked for years about expanding."

"Yes…I can see why Daddy Eddie would like this idea."

"You, too. You can move on, start something new. Creating new business has always been your forte."

Studying her, he couldn't really tell what she was thinking, but she definitely looked intrigued. Her blue eyes had widened, the irises darker in the low light, almost black against her delicate flowery skin. The shawl was still draped around her, but it had slipped from her shoulders and settled against her bare arms. For a moment, as he leaned forward, hoping to encourage a positive response, his eyes landed on the chain she always wore. He was close enough that he could almost read the engraving, which said Remember the Time.

She and Susannah had bought the charms years ago, and whenever the women felt they were making a lasting memory, they'd touch the identical pendants they wore and say the words together, "Remember the Time."

Closing the folder, she stared at it, and when she glanced up, her eyes were warmer, catching the light. "So…Daddy Eddie sent you?"

If he said yes, she wouldn't think he'd come for personal reasons, which might be good, since she didn't seem to have missed him much. But if he said no, she'd guess Lee Polls was in trouble, which would hurt his position, in terms of negotiation. She'd think Robby was working behind Daddy Eddie's back, to put together a deal to save the company. Then she'd worry about her father, too, and both Daddy Eddie and Robby would look weak.

"Yes. Your father sent me."

"Spineless," she spat, her look suddenly skewering Robby. "He couldn't bring the deal to me, himself?"

So she'd just been stringing him along. In reality, she was livid. Dammit, in negotiation with a man, Robby would have been on his toes, but Ellie always threw him off his game. "It's my deal, Ellie."

"No." She shook her head furiously. "This has got Daddy's name written all over it."

"Be that as it may," Robby said soothingly, "it's a good deal. For you and him. And me," he added.

"Really?" Swiftly, she rose and closed the space between them, standing in front of his chair. Too late, she seemed to realize she'd come too near…so near that in a gesture, he could grasp her hands and pull her into his lap.

Heat flooded him as he imagined her legs parting for him. So easily she could straddle him, squeezing his thighs with hers as the most intimate core of her settled where he could feel himself getting hard.

It had been too long since he'd held her and he craved the sweet, shuddering rush of relief that only Ellie could bring. Memories of her lovemaking claimed him, how she could get so hot for him, so slick and wet. One of her lush legs had wedged between his two jean-clad thighs, and as if knowing what he was thinking, she now tried to readjust her shawl, to cover herself, but the ends of the silk merely traced his hand, making his fingers itch to grasp and tug.

Her voice was low and throaty, belying the subject, sexy beyond what could keep his greedy hands in check. "Did you expect me to take this deal, Robby?"

"No," he answered honestly, tilting back his head and lifting his gaze from eye level to her tempting, curving hips. Peering into her eyes, he said, "But you seemed interested."

"And Daddy sent you?"

He hesitated. "Yes."

A second later, her arm swung downward, so quickly that the silk shawl slapped his cheek. Then the file folder hit him squarely in the chest. "Well, then, the answer is no," she bit out, her tone venomous. "And get out."

His hand had closed over the folder instinctively. Just as involuntarily, he rose to his feet, then recalled how close they were. Everything touched at once, and warmth rushed through him at the contact. Her breasts hit his chest. Their bellies and hips brushed and tingled. She stepped back quickly, but she'd registered his growing arousal. Ellie damn well knew every inch of him—enough to know how he felt hard, and soft, and everything in between.

Right now, he was in between. "Ellie," he whispered hoarsely, her name escaping his lips on a rush of longing.

"Don't," she said simply.

But it was too late. Reaching behind himself, he tossed the file into the chair and caught one of her arms. A handful of the silk wrap glided beneath his hand like water, but it didn't feel as soft as her bare skin. Nor as arousing as the fluttering on the surface of her skin, the shakiness of her breath.

"Get out," she whispered in soft repetition, her breath so close it fanned his cheek, smelling of after-dinner mints and coffee...

Delights she'd shared with another man. It was the wrong time to think of Percy Anders, and Robby's body hardened, his fingers tightening on her flesh with male resolve. He wanted to pull her against him and erase the other man from her mind, to feel her melt against the rock-hard wall of his body, as she'd done so many times. His lips had parted, either for a kiss, or because he didn't know what to say to her, and now he recognized how shallow his breath had become. His throat was bone-dry and his mouth felt full of sawdust. Maybe that was why his voice came out sounding even more raspy than hers.

"Would it help if I said your dad didn't send me?" he offered, stunned to realize that she'd been hiding her feelings, after all. She must have missed him. Otherwise, she wouldn't be this mad.

"I'd say you were a liar," she muttered, piercing him with a steely gaze. "But we already knew that."

"I wanted to see you, Ellie," he defended. Couldn't she feel the truth of it in the way his body was straining against hers?

"So now you've seen me. You can go."

"Dammit," he cursed, his hands now settling over both her forearms. "C'mere, Ellie." She resisted, but just barely, as he opened her arms, urging them around his waist.

The shawl slid off her shoulders and landed on the floor, and just as suddenly as her outburst, she was hugging him. Angling his face down, he nuzzled her neck, the magic clasp of her dress only inches away. She smelled like a field of flowers, turning his mind to mush.

Slowly, he backed away, now staring deeply into her eyes. She looked expectant, uncertain and wounded. So hurt that he could have ripped out his own heart. What had he put her through? Why hadn't he just taken some other job?

After all, that was the issue. Months ago, it had seemed unthinkable. Lee Polls was his life, just as surely as it was Ellie's. He'd thought the company was their future, but he knew better now. Ellie was his future. Ellie alone. Lifting a hand, he glided it upward, grazing her breast, watching the nipple contract beneath black fabric as he did so. Lightly, he traced her chin. "Look at me, baby," he whispered huskily.

Once more, he could have kicked himself for not noticing the hurt he'd put in her eyes. Pain he'd now do anything to remove. Sucking a deep breath through clenched teeth, barely able to contain his passion, he slid a hand around the column of her neck. As she tilted back her head, he glanced downward and gasped, seeing the bodice of the dress gape.

As his eyes riveted to the creamy, satiny, sloping mound of her visible breast, scalding heat raced through him. His groin tugged and his buttocks tightened, bracing against the rising tide of sensation…an ebb and flow of endless aching born on burning waves of desire.

"I'm sorry," he whispered thickly. "For everything."

Her hips lifted, seeking his, and he gasped audibly at the contact. An answering whimper tore from her throat, so needy that he knew she must be wet and drenched for him. He flicked his tongue to her neck…licking, stroking, swirling, biting. With every touch of damp heat, she pressed her hips harder, until she was moaning, writhing shamelessly, obviously wanting to climb his body and ride him.

Closing a hand over a breast, he squeezed, kneading and massaging, uttering another shuddering gasp when he did find the clasp to the bodice. As black fabric swaths came down, her breasts swung free. He fell to them, suckling hard, making her sob with longing. Even then, he didn't stop, but only nibbled the stiffened wet tips until she was whimpering like a baby.

"I need…need…"

"What?" he urged.

"Need it…" she whispered brokenly.

She didn't need to explain what "it" was. She was begging for the blistering heat of their finest moments. She needed him deep inside her, thrusting hard, losing himself to sweat and raw male exertion.

"I need it, too, Ellie," he admitted, before his mouth came down hard, finding hers and covering it with a crushing kiss. A kiss wild with contrition and remorse as his hands glided under her backside. Cupping her buttocks, he lifted her into his arms, and as he did so, her pelvis met the space between his legs. Already he was engorged, the touch explosive. He moaned as the blessed salvation of her legs wrapped around his waist, then tightened like a vise.

"I've needed it for a long time," he muttered, cradling her, somehow astonished that she still felt as light as a feather in his embrace. "Every night since you've been gone, Ellie."

She was panting hard, her hot, fluttering breath urgent against his ear. "Then give it to me, Robby."

"Yes," he said simply, now confessing this was all he'd really flown here to find. To hell with business. Pleasure, too. All he really wanted was his home. And home was wherever he found Ellie Lee.

7

ELLIE KNEW BETTER than to surrender, but the bulging muscles of Robby's biceps were too overpowering as his arms encircled her, the hard male scent of him too disturbingly pungent. She felt like a drugged zombie, or a hypnotized sleepwalker lost in a dream, powerless but to follow the lead of this man. As much as she'd been loathe to admit it, she'd missed him, craved his touch for months, and now she could only follow the dictates of whatever was most carnal within them both.

As she tightened her legs around his waist, more securely locking her ankles behind his back, he began carrying her toward the open door to the bedroom and she gasped.

His whisper was ragged against her cheek. "What?"

"Nothing," she said, but she was experiencing sensations of pure bliss, wreathing her arms around his neck and clinging as he walked, feeling his hard, honed body crushing against her. Months before, he'd taken her to hell, and now, just by this unspoken promise of passion, he was taking her to heaven, too.

It had been so long since physical pleasure had been hers to enjoy, and all night, Percy Anders had conjured memories of Robby, reminding her of what she'd been missing.

And then, he'd shown up at her front door! Just like that! Oh, she'd been shocked to see him in New York, and furious and disappointed when he'd admitted her father had sent him.

Still, this was a fantasy come true. Right now, she wanted him with every fiber of her being. He'd betrayed her, yes, just as her father had. But she simply couldn't fight the flood of desire taking flight inside her. Her soul was soaring.

She'd tried to be standoffish, hoping he'd get the message and leave, yet…

It had been hopeless. This was Robby, after all. She'd always been responsive to him, open emotionally and physically. Her legs wrapped more tightly around him, her fully exposed pelvis, the lower lips so open, delightfully pressing his abdomen. Her freed, bare breasts were swaying, brushing his chest in a way that was excruciating. It tantalized and aroused. Her sensitized nipples chaffed the rough cotton of his Western shirt, making her whimper. Every inch of her body yearned for the soothing, medicinal salve of his wet mouth, and better, the heady plunge when he finally stripped off his jeans, removed her panties and got between her legs.

Another moan was released from between her parted lips as she offered a smattering of kisses along his jaw. Panting, she realized she was shaking all over. She wanted him, and call her spoiled, but Ellie was used to getting what she wanted. Later, she'd just thank him for a lovely evening, then say goodbye, right? It was really that simple. For now…

She whimpered once more. Feeling brazen, she shimmied her behind, forcing her hips to slip downward on his warm belly. Registering heat and contact, she cried out, her pelvis quivering until she knew she couldn't stand another moment of this hot anticipation zinging along her nerve endings. Everything felt so right. The sexy, soft piano music, the dim, flattering light, the warming temperature of the room. In just a moment, she was going to be even more aroused and feel close to coming. Then he'd hold her tight, and she would come, curled in his arms.

Oh, before that, she was going to make this man really hot, though. So crazy horny that he'd always remember she was his best lover. She couldn't wait to see his facial expression when she'd pushed him beyond all human limits—his glazed eyes narrowed, his breath coming in spurts, his mouth uttering little needy whispers.

Now, he slid a splayed hand down her thigh and roughly pushed her dress upward, then he urgently rubbed brisk circles on her leg, seemingly reveling in the silken touch of the stockings. He gasped when he felt her bare flesh and garters.

"No panty hose," he ascertained, his voice husky, his throat seemingly dry from panting.

"Nope."

Gasping as the dress hem bunched around her waist, he'd left nothing between them but the silk of her panties and the threadbare denim of his jeans. Down there, where they touched, she could feel him now, hot and throbbing, hard and ready, the head of his penis probing his jean's fly. Moisture gushed, and while only damp before, her panties became drenched. Seconds before she'd been on a precipice, but now the contact pushed her over the edge, and she was racing toward a place that was new, strange and indefinable, falling into a wild cascade of fervent heat.

That hot hand tightened beneath her, grasping her bottom, squeezing, urging her to rock against his erection, to ride him. He punctuated his moves with short, frustrated male grunts of uncompromising need. She answered with strangled sighs, trusting his hands not to drop her as she bucked against him, her silken panties providing the needed slick lubrication as she glided up, then down. She wanted his pants gone so badly now.

"Oh…" she whispered, her breath catching in her throat. "Oh…oh…"

"What, baby?"

"This…" Her mind focused on the steely, blistering-hot ridge that was further engorging…splitting her lower folds completely and gliding between, feeling so hot and wet and slippery. He'd explode with just a few more touches. He was that ready. There was no turning back. She'd been drowning in his embrace, and now she swooned at the renewed friction, making her want to ride him harder, wild and fast—her hair flying, her breasts bouncing, her hips writhing, each hair-trigger movement threatening to be the last before she came.

Damn, she thought, heat exploding inside her. Robby's stupid hands were staying her, holding her back from the much-needed release. She was champing at the bit from the infernal teasing, feeling downright desperate.

And yet she didn't want this sensation to end. Yes, she thought, he could walk all the way to the moon and back with her in his arms. The ridge that was probing her panties felt good…so unbelievably good. More so, since he was thrusting harder now, pushing between her legs, guiding her faster—up and down, up and down—until her concentration shattered. Her whole body was taut, coiled and tense for the orgasm his body promised was coming soon….

But then he stopped moving.

"Please…" The hoarse whisper tore from her throat as scalding heat flooded her. Everything seemed a blur. When had her shawl dropped to the floor? And the hook that held up her dress bodice really come undone? When had her sensitive core begun crying out for satisfaction? This was just like Robby. He always got her all wound up and toyed with her. All he cared about was power and control.

"You're starting to get so hot," he said in a playful drawl as she sucked an audible breath through clenched teeth.

"You make me want it so badly," she gasped.

"It?"

"You know."

"I think I do." He leaned close to steal a wild, fast kiss, his tongue plundering, then tracing her neck and bare shoulders, feeling luscious. His free hand caught a breast from beneath, stroked the silken curve, then he lifted the mound, his long fingers curling over it as he raised it to his warm, panting mouth. Leaning back a fraction, to get his bearings, he suckled, a movement that forced his hips to slam to hers, locking them and sending fire into her extremities.

"I thought you'd keep fighting me, Ellie," he murmured.

How could she? His mouth was working magic; he drew tantalizing circles with his tongue, then teased the nipple and bit sweetly. Suddenly, he suckled, and she couldn't find her breath to answer him. His body was as hard as granite. Between his legs, he was harder still, and through his increasingly tight jeans, she could feel each inch pulsing as he drew a nipple hard between his lips. Below, he was straining and rigid with unrelieved need, so even his jeans were soaked with her juices now. Her breasts were aching.

"I *should* fight you," she managed, her voice shaking.

His tongue was flicking a taut bud. "Why?"

"Because of what you do to me," she muttered, her hand grappling between them, fishing for the hem of his shirt and finding it just as they reached the couch-bed. Catching a fistful of cotton, she tugged. Pearl-studded snaps flew open, and the next thing she knew, she was groaning, her face nuzzling deep, burrowing in soft chest hair. Her hands molded around massive shoulders, then she opened her fists, splayed her fingers and grasped his pectorals, massaging. Angling her head down, she played tit for tat, capturing a knotted, stiff male nipple, nibbling and chewing until he uttered a guttural cry.

His head reared back. Fingers thrust upward from her neck, driving deeply into her hair and grabbing the strands in fistfuls. Encouraged, she suckled harder, raking her teeth across the nipple, then she gushed again when she felt him throb between her legs. He exhaled shakily as shivers spun through her blood.

"I missed you so much," he rasped, his broad chest puffed out, the better to take the ministrations of her tongue. Using just the flickering wet tip, she traced a final circle around the taut peak. "I want you to show me exactly what you missed, Robby," she panted.

"Everything," he promised.

"Like what?"

"Everything," he whispered

"Then show me. Every single thing. Let's do it all."

Somehow, he was still standing, holding her. With her legs stretched around him, she was shaking all over as he stroked her breast once more, pinching a bud and making molten fire whirl inside her. Burning liquid danced, plunging from somewhere unexpected. It knotted between her legs, clustering right at her core, then dissolved into a tiny mass of sizzling nerve endings that had to come undone very soon, leaving her praying she'd come….

"You're making me feel crazy," she muttered, half insane with need, jittery and confused and hot.

It was just like old times. She was suspended on the brink, hovering over heaven, and always at his mercy. His tongue was wild on her breast now, the touch quivering, scalding and wet.

"Robby, put me down," she muttered, frustrated when her hips ground against him, but he suddenly shifted away, arranging her in his arms so that her seeking wet core couldn't touch what she most wanted.

"Don't," she muttered. "C'mon…I want more."

"Me, too."

"Then give it to me." Again, she writhed, twisting in his

arms and seeking him, but he denied the touch and only leaned lithely and laid her gently on the foldout couch. She sank onto the covers, her unquenched desire a burdensome thirst. She needed him in the bed…bringing her off. If their past was any indication, he'd do so many times before this night was done.

"Now…" she demanded.

He offered a sexy half smile. His tongue stretched, licking his lips as if his mouth had gone dry. He stared down at her. "Naughty, naughty," he murmured with a soft chuckle.

"You know it."

"I like to see you like this, Ellie…wanting me so bad…"

Her hungry eyes roved over his body as she reached to touch his thigh. The worn jeans felt like silk as she ran a splayed palm over his thigh. The bunched muscles were firm, and his hips suddenly thrust forward.

She was lucky. Some women never found such a perfect lover. Robby's body fit her like a hand in a glove. It was just too bad he'd broken contact, leaving her lying on the bed bereft; without his, her whole body was mourning the loss. He moaned as her hand caressed his inner thigh, then glided over his pant's fly. When her fingers closed around the shaft, he surged, his weight pressing against the mattress as if he needed to brace and steady himself.

"I love the way you touch me," he whispered.

Her hand shaking, she undid the snap of his jeans, then managed to drag down the zipper, her own excitement rising when he gasped. He was fully engorged, thrusting through the fly, and her hand moved quickly, fondling him, touching him thoroughly through his briefs, studying each nuance. Arching his hips, he shuddered as she massaged.

"Ah…" He sucked in an audible breath. "Oh…"

Words had left him. She knew he was hanging on by only a thread. With a free hand, she grasped his fingers, and drew his hand down, too, thrusting it between her legs. Suddenly, he leaned, swooping down to slam his hot mouth to hers, the lips insistent and unforgiving; meantime, he touched her panties, registering soaked silk.

Crouching lower then, he deepened the kiss, pushing his hot tongue between her lips, until her mouth felt bruised and swollen. She masturbated him and he her, then he opened her garters, dragging down her stockings. His mouth still on hers, his hand fell to her panties once more and a finger suddenly entered her, pushing inside, taking the wet silk with it, the finger carrying her moisture; pulling it out, he slowly strummed her clitoris, pushing her toward her release.

"Get me off," she muttered, panting. "Please, Robby…"

"All night," he promised.

"No…not all night. Now, now!"

"Come on, baby," he urged, his voice low, commanding, as he shifted his own pelvis away, denying her touch. His tongue probed her lips, then her mouth turned more pliable. One hand cupped her face, a thumb tracing her jaw, guiding the kiss, plundering.

His other hand was busier, probing her clitoris, circling it wild and fast through the drenched silk of her underwear. She didn't care that he hadn't touched flesh yet. It hardly mattered. Gasping, she lifted her hips, straining for the touch. Everything went blank. Her mind shattered. She felt so wet…everywhere. Then she burst. It was like a brilliant sun crashing, and as she came, memories exploded inside her…

She had to strip him now, blindly reaching for him as palpitations rocked her body. She had to kiss every inch of him, suckle between his legs until he was blind with lust. Even as her hands were still seeking him, he grasped the waistband of her panties, pulling them down, then her dress was gone, too, and he stepped back to view his handiwork. She was breathless, her heart pounding a steady tattoo.

He smiled. "How was that for starters, Ellie?"

"Some people finish there. But not you."

"No." He shook his head slowly, a smile tilting his lips. "Not me, sweetheart."

Blue slits of eyes surveyed her bare breasts with a proprietary air before taking in her belly and hips. Backlit by illumination from the living room, he seemed to tower above her, maybe because a giant shadow was cast on the wall behind him. He looked almost like a giant, so tall and muscular, his wind-tossed dark hair a little wild. He was so good-looking…the chiseled jaw and high cheekbones and almost decadently sensual lips belying his lowly birth. Her eyes settled on his chest as he shrugged out of the shirt, drinking in the narrowing sexy pelt that raced toward where she'd opened his pants.

She sucked in another steadying breath, her whole body aching when she saw the white sliver of his briefs, hiding the bulge in the crevice of his open fly. In the months they'd been apart, she hadn't exactly forgotten the heady sensuality that drew her to the man, but she was reminded of it as his gaze pinned her and he kicked off his shoes. As he stepped out of his remaining clothes, she wondered what she'd been thinking. How could she have left Banner, Mississippi? Shouldn't she get up right now, pack her bags and prepare to go home?

As he came toward her, she shook off the feelings, her eyes fixed to the most male part of him. Fully aroused, he looked gorgeous, protruding from a rich bed of hair. Definitely, with him naked in the room, it seemed the wrong time to experience anything but lust. And yet she felt homesick. She wished they could make love, just as in the old days, then dress and drive to Clancy's place for a late-night snack. Her heart squeezed. If they made it through the night without starving, they would have been able to go to Delia's Diner the next morning. Ellie could see J.D. and Susannah, too. Pain immediately sliced through her. Maybe she'd even call a truce with Daddy Eddie. That would make her mom so happy....

Heaven knew, Ellie and her dad had experienced countless scuffles over the years, since Ellie was every bit as hard-headed as Daddy Eddie. And Ellie's mother didn't deserve to have her beloved family torn apart. Patricia Lee's whole life revolved around family, and whenever relationships were out of whack, she never rested until they were repaired. Painful emotions twisted inside Ellie once more, and now, totally against her will, she thought back to J.D.'s funeral.

Her mother had urged Ellie to make up with Daddy Eddie. Ellie just wished she'd been able to discuss the matter with Robby, since in addition to becoming her lover, he'd become her very best friend, but then she'd been businesslike with him, since she was fighting with him, too. Susannah had been mourning J.D., of course. And those few days were, perhaps, the loneliest Ellie had ever experienced in her life.

As Robby slid next to her in bed, she reminded herself that he'd betrayed her, and now his gorgeous face turned strangely pensive, as if to say he'd picked up on her shift in mood. Not that it surprised her. When it came to her emotions, Robby had a sixth sense, a radar he possessed just for her. Except when it came to her feelings about being president of Lee Polls, of course.

Nevertheless, she sighed as their bodies twined, his legs falling between hers, their chests brushing. Jittery heat had ebbed, and now she merely felt warm and dreamy, even as aroused, peaking nipples touched and he lifted a finger to her cheek and trailed it downward in a gesture so simple that it nearly broke her heart. How had her life gotten so messed up? Why did hundreds of miles separate her from this man?

"What's wrong?" he asked softly.

Everything…and nothing. Shaking her head, she wasn't about to explain, but only stretched against the warmth of his body, loving the feel of his legs…each muscular contour, the rigidity of the muscles, the bristling hair. He was still hard, as excited as she, but seemingly more intent on whatever she'd been thinking.

"Nothing," she replied, her breath just a bit steadier than it had been moments before.

"No…talk to me."

Shaking her head, she arched her hips, silently letting him feel her heat as she settled hands on his shoulders, sensations careening through her. She'd always loved his shoulders. It was a silly thing, but they were so big and strong, the skin smooth beneath her touch. Her voice turned husky once more. "There are things I'd rather do."

His smile was slow and lazy, a seductive smile that twisted the corners of his mouth upward in such a heart-stopping way that it always took her breath. With his face so close, she could see every nuance, a sudden twinkle in the blue irises, the passing of cloudier emotions as he flattened a hand and settled it on her waist. Slowly, as he blew out a shivery-sounding sigh, he palmed her skin, then glided a hand over her hip and down a thigh, his gaze following the flow of his hand.

"Maybe we should talk," he murmured, the drawl dropping a near octave.

She shook her head once more. "There's no need, Robby. We've said everything we need to say."

"And then some."

She didn't want to be reminded. Lifting her finger, she pressed it to his lips to silence him, and his eyes met hers again. "I want you," she whispered. "And you want me. So there's not a whole lot to discuss."

It wasn't strictly true, and they both knew it. In the long pause that followed, all the unsaid words seemed to hang between them in the balance, and then, as if he could no longer hold back, he leaned so near that his breath fanned her cheek. Tilting his head, he angled it downward. His lips settled on hers, pressed, then the kiss deepened, turning hotter and more penetrating.

While walking between the front room and here, he'd obviously experienced a rush of passion, but now he was able to control it once more. Sighing, she leaned her head back, enjoying the kiss—how he stoked embers like a master fire-builder, poking and prodding the kindling.

And then she ignited. Her mind turned hazy once more, the thoughts about home taking a backseat to the joy of the kiss as his tongue explored. The heat that claimed her was building more intensely now, more purposefully. Lifting her hips, thrusting, she gasped and glided a hand over the back of his to bring his hand to her groin, urging it between her legs. "Touch me some more."

"Okay," he whispered.

She was naked now, so it wasn't like before, and he offered a soft sound of satisfaction as he cupped her, then stroked the exposed flesh, the backs of his hands smoothing her inner thighs. A finger dipped, then plunged. He pushed inside, seemingly reveling in the feel—all slick, tight velvet. Whatever guttering desire she'd experienced reignited as he kneeled above her. His eyes were hungrier now—sweeping her body, studying her face as he fondled her intimately.

"You're so wet." He spoke tenderly.

"Make me come again, Robby," she pleaded. "You know just what to do, how to touch me."

"Any man would."

That was a lie, but she didn't refute it. "Maybe."

He chuckled softly, as if to say he knew better, and the sound of his voice was like music. Using two fingers, he held them rigidly, then slowly pushed them inside her, twisting them until she cried out. He asked, "What are you going to do for me, sweetheart?"

Raising her arms, she clasped her hands behind her head, relaxing to better take the pleasure he was offering. "I'll think of something."

"And what do you most want me to do to you?"

He was doing it now. "I don't care," she managed, her breath catching as he pushed both fingers deeper inside, testing where she was gushing, turning to burning liquid. His other hand, feeling suddenly insistent, further pushed apart her upper thighs. "Let me see everything," he said, his voice as low as the piano music from the next room. "All of you. Every bit, Ellie."

Shifting her weight, she sighed shakily and crooked her knee, then was rewarded to see his gaze sharpen, to hear his breath catch raggedly.

"Oh, Ellie," he whispered. "I missed you so much…"

"Don't talk," she whispered back, her hips moving in an age-old rhythm as his fingers snuck deeper inside her, sweetly stroking her ridges, curling for her G-spot.

Abruptly, he stopped, and she gasped in protest, but he only leaned closer. She could see his nostrils flare, and when he placed a soft, gentle kiss on her lips, then leaned away once more, to look at her, she blew out another, longer audible breath. He planted peppering kisses everywhere on her neck, her shoulders, her jaw. She felt a wet, deep kiss land on her chin, and as her arms wrapped around his neck, he lay fully on top of her. His mouth found hers once more, his tongue pushing inside her mouth, swirling.

As if in a dream, she stretched her tongue for more of a kiss, registering how he settled into her embrace, his skin damp with perspiration. She was hot, shaking with sex as one of his knees urged hers to move upward, so he could gain better access. A second later, she felt the head of his penis…probing, seeking, insisting. It dipped inside her, carring a wonderful burning sensation that nearly destroyed her. Then she took in a fraction more and he thrust splayed hands into her hair. Spread fingers glided against her scalp, feeling like heaven right before he grasped the strands in fistfuls.

His mouth turned slower on hers, more languid as he simultaneously braced himself on his elbows. Never breaking the kiss, he moved his hips, pushing inside another scant inch, opening and filling her, then another inch, another. He seemed to be making sure he had his bearings, setting his rhythm, and her hips encouraged, meeting him. It was as if she was silently begging until he satisfied her anew, each thrust offering another hint of the total pleasure she craved.

He was hotter than she'd ever felt him…bigger than she remembered. Even just hovering near her, he felt huge, and her mind blanked once more, her eyes shutting, her head tilting back as she silently waited. Suddenly, his mouth on hers stilled. His hands tightened in her hair and his body went taut. All at once, he thrust hard and deep, pushing into her with his full weight, the movement shocking and abrupt, making her gasp, stretching her beyond what she'd known was possible.

And then they were gone. Lights seemed to extinguish. Sounds ceased except for their breathing. Her arms tightened around him and she clung and rode, letting him push her to the edge until she was tumbling over it again, only to be brought back to the precipice. Locked in a state of sheer oblivion, she was finally reduced to quivering nerves, and only then did his arms tighten around her, too. He hugged her so close that not a breath could pass between them, then his body pounded hers, taking her to even bolder heights, until he gushed inside her, rocking against her until he was fully spent.

She swooned, her body limp. After a moment, he sighed heavily. Untangling his limbs from hers, he leaned back a fraction, his eyes following the motion of his hand as it trailed slowly down the long trajectory of her body. Surveying her rose-toned flesh, which was reddened from heat and damp with perspiration, he blew out a long, almost sad-sounding sigh. His hand stilled near her hip and he gave her sensitive flesh a gentle pat, then he sighed once more and rose from the mattress.

Squinting, she watched him circle the couch-bed, and when she tried to speak, she realized her throat was too raw. Clearing it, she then licked her lips, amazed at how dry they felt. "What are you doing?" she murmured.

Now he was grabbing his briefs from the floor and thrusting his long legs into them. Shaking out his jeans, he stepped into those, too. As much as she could admire his perfect balance as he put on his socks, then stepped into his shoes, she still wasn't quite sure what he was doing. Not even when he leaned with agility, lifted his shirt from the floor and began shrugging into it.

"What?" she ventured again, still squinting. "Are you hungry or something?"

He was snapping the shirt now. "No. But I better go."

"Go?"

"Back to the hotel."

"You got a hotel?"

"Yeah."

"Then why did you bring that bag?"

He shrugged. "I don't know."

She struggled to a sitting position, starting to wish she was getting dressed, too. Somehow, clothes gave a person an advantage, she decided, now shaking the duvet free and wrapping it around her shoulders, not that it helped. Besides, she was still blistering hot and coated with sweat.

"I'd better go," he said. "This shouldn't have happened."

"But you're the one who started it."

"No way."

"I didn't do anything."

"You wore that dress."

"Well, it wasn't on purpose. It's not like I knew you were coming over."

"Exactly."

"What's that supposed to mean?"

"You had a date."

It was over, though. And it sure hadn't stopped Robby from coming on to her. She shook her head, unable to believe any of this. Everything was still sinking in. "You're leaving?" How could he, when she was still hot all over and just getting started?

Nodding, he tucked in his shirt by flattening his hand on his belly and making little jabbing motions, forcing the shirt down inside the waistband of his jeans. Dammit, even that looked good, and her own hands started itching to touch that washboard-flat belly again.

When he was completely finished dressing, he stared down at the bed, at her. "I'd really better go, Ellie."

She peered at him, slack jawed. "So you said."

"Forgive me if you're mad."

She gaped. "Forgive you? For which thing?"

"I know," he muttered. "It's a long list. So just take your pick."

She crossed her arms in stunned silence, hardly caring that the motion only served to lift her bare breasts, as if for his gaze. The fool man was looking, too, his greedy eyes getting that dazed look that always plagued males when a woman's breasts were on view.

Good, she thought. Let him eat his heart out. Trouble was, his hot gaze was getting her all excited again, too. Because of that, she wasn't at all happy when her body betrayed her and her nipples suddenly puckered.

"Here," she huffed. "I'd better show you to the door."

He raised a hand, palm out, as if he were stopping traffic. "No need, sweetheart."

"Is it something I said?"

"We could have talked about a million things, Ellie. But we didn't."

No, they'd just made love.

"And that's it?" He was just going to leave?

"Yeah," he said. And with that, he pivoted, turning on his heel, and simply strode toward the living room. She was halfway off the bed before she figured out her mistake. She wasn't going to run after him! No way! Quickly, she sat back down. In the next room, he was shoving the file back into his duffel.

Damn him, she thought, embarrassed heat flooding her. Her father had sent him. That was bad enough. But once Robby had gotten here, and she'd rejected her dad's deal, he'd decided to use her for sex. Fury coursed through her. Call it a double standard, perhaps, since she'd been thinking about doing the very same thing with Robby an hour before. But how could he leave now? How could he leave after what had just happened?

The memory of his hands again, the heat of his mouth, the hard thrust of his lower body as he filled her almost had her getting to her feet. Her lips parted to call to him, to tell him to stay.

But she couldn't. He'd just used her. "Shut the door after yourself!"

Already, his hand was on the doorknob. "You'd better lock it after I'm gone."

That was rich. "I don't need you to worry about my safety, Robby Robriquet! I've been fine, all by myself in New York! Without you!" She just wished the fool man hadn't left her body burning.

She wasn't even sure he'd heard. Already, the door had opened and shut. And her ex-lover, who'd just become her lover again, was gone.

"What just happened!" she exclaimed. Why had she fallen for that? Let him make love to her as if they'd never been apart? Hopping out of bed, she muttered, "So he thinks he can walk in here and start using me for business, or sex, or both?"

Suddenly shrugging off the duvet around her shoulders, she headed for the closet. She wasn't about to let him get away with this, no, sir. A woman had to have some self-respect.

8

"I GUESS I CAN ADD that to the long list of things I hate about New York," Robby muttered as he stood on the sidewalk, shifted the duffel on his shoulder, then shoved his hands deeply into his jeans pockets and tried to regroup. It was hard to do since he could still smell Ellie's scent on his skin. "Practically everybody in this city looks like a thug."

Sighing, he stared at two goons in a dark sedan across the street from Ellie's apartment. Because of guys like that, he hated to think of Ellie in this huge city, all by herself. As a car passed, headlights shined in such a way that Robby could make out the features of the two men in the sedan. Yeah, they definitely looked like small-time hoods. Feeling uncharacteristic apprehension, Robby glanced over his shoulder. Ellie's apartment looked dark, since the blinds were drawn. Should he return and make sure she'd locked up?

Shaking his head, he decided against it. First, the two guys weren't all that dangerous-looking. Probably, they were working for a car service and just waiting for their next call. Besides, Ellie was a lot of things, but she wasn't stupid, which meant she'd locked the door already. She'd made a point of not seeing him outside or saying goodbye, and he didn't blame her.

When she'd opened the door, wearing that hot little black cocktail number, he'd been powerless but to go to bed with her. The sparks she generated would always make him want her, so could he help it if his raging hormones had taken over? From the second he'd laid eyes on her, he'd known he wouldn't be satisfied until the dress was in a puddle around her feet.

Now he had to get out of here, though. As soon as he'd entered the apartment, he'd realized Ellie had built a whole new, very successful life. He'd been blown away by how tastefully her apartment had been decorated. It had looked lived in, too, as if she had no plans to return to Banner anytime soon.

Unbelievable. Months ago, she'd hopped out of bed with him, said a hasty goodbye and had been gone by nightfall. Overnight, she'd changed his world. Deep down, on the morning she'd left, Robby had assumed they'd just had a fight like any other. It was the worst fight to that point in their relationship, at least judging by Ellie's tone; still, he'd figured she'd cool off, then return and make up with him.

She hadn't come to work on Monday, though. By noon, Patricia had called Daddy Eddie saying that, in turn, Ellie had called her from New York, saying she wanted Patricia to care for her house, since she'd already left town. Unable to believe it, Robby had driven over, half expecting Ellie to be home. She wasn't, however, and through a window, he'd seen empty drawers and the door to an empty closet gaping open.

For days after that, Robby had felt stunned, unable to believe Ellie could have left town just like that, with complete disregard for his feelings. He'd never do that to her.

But he had, hadn't he? a voice niggled. Or something just as bad, since he'd known how much she'd coveted the head job at Lee Polls. It was her birthright, after all, and she'd had every reason to expect the spot would be hers.

Still…call it wishful thinking, but all this time, Robby had imagined Ellie living out of boxes and maybe feeling depressed. Not that he'd expected to see tissues everywhere, or boxes of chocolate, or bags attesting to how much she'd been shopping, but he'd expected some evidence of turmoil, some tiny hint that she'd missed him.

Instead, she'd been living beautifully, if frugally, and using her place as both a residence and an office. No doubt, she'd been eating at Susannah's restaurant regularly, as well. That, too, was a fine-looking establishment, warm and cozy, with inviting, intimate tables and Susannah's name blazed across the window in gold. So much for the idea that Ellie had been suffering the sleepless nights that had so plagued Robby.

At any rate, Daddy Eddie and Patricia would be happy to hear Ellie was doing fine. Proud, too. No matter how accomplished Ellie became, she'd always be their baby girl. Feeling another surge of pique, Robby pursed his lips. Didn't Ellie care about any of them? Daddy Eddie and Patricia had been worried sick, not that Daddy Eddie would admit it.

Yet Ellie was oblivious to their concern. Banner, Mississippi, was the furthest cry from her mind. By comparison, New York overwhelmed Robby somewhat, but it hadn't fazed his ex in the least. She'd even found a new man. Against his will, Robby felt another rush of temper, which he tried and failed to squelch. How could she stand Percy Anders? She'd invited him inside after their date, too, and the man had stayed longer than Robby had liked. Had they kissed good-night?

"Man, I hope not," he muttered. Sighing, he did a double take. Something about the black, four-door sedan was still bothering him. He thought once more about making sure Ellie had locked the door, but only because he was a protective fool.

And that made him an idiot. Ellie didn't need him. She didn't want him. Romance was over between them. She'd looked so gorgeous tonight and for another man. Percy Anders hadn't seemed like much to look at, but Robby believed in statistics. Math was Ellie's forte, too, and since numbers never lied, it seemed Percy might be the right man for her. Ellie had done her homework, no doubt, while searching for The One.

"Damn," Robby muttered now, shaking his head as if to clear it of confusion and starting for the curb. Glad to see a cab, he raised an arm and felt a wave of relief when the driver seemed to spot him. As the cab veered toward him, a need for flight seized Robby once more, just as it had moments before while he was still in bed. Oh, feeling Ellie snuggled against him had felt like heaven, and he'd wanted to stay all night, but he couldn't bring himself to do so.

Yes, a man had to keep things straight in his mind. His and Ellie's shared passion tonight meant they were merely scratching an itch. Where he'd be willing to change his work life if she'd have him back, she'd moved on to another life. For an instant, he imagined himself packing his bags in Banner and moving to New York, to live with her, but that was crazy.

"She's moved on," he muttered out loud. And more than anything, that fact made him want to get out of here—out of her bed, off her street, out of her town. Too bad her hot taste was still on his lips, all peppermint-and-coffee. He could smell her, too, the perfume rich, complex and enticing. Elsewhere, he felt a little sticky, still warmed by her juices, and although he tried not to dwell on the sensation, he couldn't help himself and shuddered.

Blowing out another sigh, he stared at where the cab had stopped across the intersection for a red light, feeling glad he'd gotten a hotel room. As he'd left it earlier, he'd decided to bring the duffel, in case he'd wound up spending the night with Ellie. Sure, he'd told himself he'd brought it only because it contained the folder for the business deal he'd proposed, but that had been a lie.

"C'mon," he murmured as the light changed and the cab crossed the street, heading toward him. "Finally."

Opening the door, he tossed his duffel onto the seat, then slid next to it. "The Washington Square Hotel," he said.

"Sounds good," the cabbie commented.

As soon as he got there, Robby told himself he was going to check out. To hell with spending a lonesome night in a strange, cold bed. For a minute, he considered telling the cabbie to head for the airport, instead. He could cancel the room by phone, then eat while waiting for another flight. Wincing, he bit back a curse. He searched his memory. Hadn't he removed his shaving kit from the duffel? Left it on the lip of the sink? He was sure he had....

What a jerk. Well, he could always buy another. Taking a deep breath, he puffed his cheeks and exhaled. No, he should go to the hotel and check the room, just to make sure he'd left nothing else behind. Well, leave it to Ellie to scramble his thoughts. She hadn't even gone for the business deal, although it would have been advantageous for her. Lee Polls needed it, too. They'd survive, but this deal would have put both companies solidly in the black. "So that's how much she doesn't want to deal with me, or her dad," he muttered.

"What?"

He glanced at the cabbie. "Just talking to myself."

"Bad habit."

"Only if you answer."

Returning to his thoughts, he wished Ellie could have done what was good for business, instead of acting out of spite. So much for brightening Daddy Eddie's day. An image of the old man came into Robby's mind. He liked the old codger. Ellie had always been his favorite, his little girl, the apple of his eye. Why couldn't Ellie see he was trying to do what was best for her, in whatever a misguided way?

A slight smile tilted Robby's lips. Daddy Eddie often

talked about Robby and Ellie getting together, but only because he didn't think there was a snowball's chance in hell of it happening. Months ago, when Daddy Eddie had first pulled Robby aside and offered him the promotion, Robby had thought Daddy Eddie knew about the affair. Now he no longer thought so.

But was he certain? Daddy Eddie was one slippery fellow. The only thing more elusive was his daughter. Swallowing hard, Robby tried not to think about her, but even now, he could feel her soft, silken hair as strands teased the spaces between his fingers…before he touched her full, lush breasts, the tips aroused for his touch.

He missed her friendship as much as he craved her body. He'd wanted to talk to her about her old man and catch her up on all the town gossip. In addition to what he'd told her, J.D. and Susannah were doing just fine, and while neither had said a word, Robby guessed they were trying to get pregnant now. Of course, Susannah and Ellie talked on the phone, so as far as Robby knew, Ellie knew that. But maybe not. And did she know that Sheriff Kemp and Delia from Delia's Diner were dating steadily now?

Or that Charlie was out of jail? Robby cringed. Besides seeing Ellie, that was the other reason he'd wanted to get out of Banner. So far, he'd avoided his old man, but Banner wasn't as big as a postage stamp, so it was only a matter of time until he and Charlie came face-to-face.

However, maybe the old man had learned something in prison. Maybe he'd figured out it was in his best interest to stay away from his son. For a second, Robby thought of the girl Charlie had killed, Shirley Fey. She'd been trying hard against the odds. Her folks hadn't had much money, but plenty of love to spread around. Since their daughter's death, Robby had seen them in town, too, the light snuffed from their eyes.

Even eight years down the pike, the two grieving parents still seemed like shells of their former selves.

They, too, would run into Charlie eventually. Dammit, if only his father would just leave town. But how could he, when that would probably violate his parole? Fortunately, the cabbie was pulling in front of the entrance to the hotel. Digging into his pocket, Robby found some bills and held them over the seat, so the driver could take them.

"Keep the change," said Robby.

"Generous of you."

Maybe, but as he got out of the cab and slammed the door, Robby wasn't feeling generous at all. In fact, he felt stingy as hell. He wanted to turn right back around, drive to Ellie's and storm inside. He wanted to make her belong to him, and him alone. He sure didn't want to share with Percy Anders.

"Which is why you've got to get out of town," he uttered as the cab pulled away from the curb. On the one hand, he thought of Ellie, only a mile away. On the other, he thought of Charlie, whom he'd see, no doubt, after he returned to Banner. And then, heaving a sigh, Robbie shifted the strap of the duffel on his shoulder, headed up some stairs and pushed through the door of the hotel.

He never saw the black sedan that had followed him.

"THAT'S FUNNY," Ellie murmured. Pausing between two sets of double doors, in the vestibule leading to the hotel lobby, she craned her neck around. Two men had just exited. One was physically larger than the other; both were wearing leather coats and heading toward the black sedan they'd parked at the curb. They must have seen her, but neither offered a glance, almost as if they didn't want to be noticed.

Still…her cab had followed their sedan here, and now, as it turned out, the two men had come inside the hotel, too, if only for a moment. It couldn't be a coincidence. Had they followed Robby?

When she caught a glimpse of herself in a mirror, her thoughts ended abruptly. She groaned. She had Robby to thank, of course, for how ridiculous she looked. Moving hurriedly in the dim light of her apartment, she'd grabbed jeans and a T-shirt, but now she realized the shirt, worn under a rumpled raincoat, was turned inside out and that the socks, which were visible in back since she'd worn clog-style shoes, didn't match.

She hadn't had time to brush her hair, and the dark strands were a mess, flying every which way from where Robby had thrust his hands into a tangled mass. He'd eaten off her lipstick with his kisses, and her mascara was no longer fresh, leaving slight smudges under her eyes. She didn't look like a raccoon, thankfully, but she did look as if she'd just gotten out of bed, which of course, she had. Quickly, she pushed away the recollections of how good making love with Robby had felt. It was difficult though, since she still felt hot from what he'd been doing to her.

She glanced a final time toward the dark sedan as it pulled away from the curb. Maybe it wasn't the same car that had been parked near her apartment, after all. From her window, she'd seen Robby get into a cab, then managed to catch up to him in another cab and tail him. The sedan had stayed behind Robby's car most of the way, but at one point traffic got heavy and she could no longer see it.

Surely, she was mistaken about the car, she thought, as she headed through the next interior door to the lobby proper. It was a small hotel, red carpeted with mirrored walls and a long counter. The young man behind it was tall, thin and gangly, and judging from his age and the textbook he was reading, he was probably a university student.

Wishing she looked a little less disheveled, Ellie strode to the counter, suddenly wondering exactly what she wanted to say. She'd been so riled that she'd just grabbed her pocketbook and bolted out the door without forethought.

The man was squinting. "Can I help you?"

"Uh…" She glanced over her shoulder once more. Before she thought it through, she said, "Those guys…"

After waiting patiently, the man then prompted, "The two men who just left?"

She nodded. "Yeah. I don't know if you can tell me, but are they registered here?"

He surveyed her for a long moment. "Why?"

"I…was coming here, uh, to see a friend, and their car was right in front of mine most of the way."

"Sorry, ma'am, I can't give out information."

Maybe not, but he'd hesitated and she couldn't help but speculate why. "Well, I'd like to see…" Her voice trailed off, and she'd had numerous things to say. They'd been swirling around in her mind on the drive over, especially since Robby had the nerve to leave as soon as they'd had sex.

She felt her cheeks flame with embarrassed heat. Sex, she thought again. Obviously, that's all the past hour or so had been to Robby, pure and simple. Intentionally, he'd used her. If she'd accepted his business offer, would it have happened?

"To see?" the man prompted again.

"Robby Robriquet," she said, aware her thoughts had drifted because of the memories of holding Robby naked in her arms. Another wave of unwanted recollection washed over her, this time of his practiced tongue at her neck. "Uh…if you can't give me his room number, could you please call him and tell him he has a guest?"

The man all but rolled his eyes, as if to say he wished Ellie could decide what she wanted. Then he riffled absently through some pages of his open book, as if to indicate he'd like to get back to his reading, and after that, he slowly dropped his gaze over her, getting a better look. Finally, he said, "You seem harmless enough. Mr. Robriquet checked in earlier tonight. He's in room three-eleven. Now, I've got to get back to my reading. Okay?"

"Thanks," she said, vaguely registering that the man had readily given Robby's room information, but had refused to divulge anything about the other two men. Now the clerk was staring at her expectantly.

"Anything else I can do for you?"

She shook her head, but couldn't bring herself to budge. What was she going to do? Go upstairs, confront Robby and…what? Her father had sent him to offer a business deal, and Robby had wanted to scratch an itch, so he'd slept with her. She'd always found him irresistible, so she'd given in. Now she felt like a fool.

Now she took a deep breath. "No, thanks for all your help," she managed to say.

And then, instead of going upstairs, Ellie turned and walked out the door again, into the soft autumn night.

"YES, SUSANNAH, I followed Robby to his hotel like an idiot," Ellie found herself saying the next day as the clock ticked toward noon. Already, she'd related the dismal details of her date with Percy Anders, the only highlight to which was the marvelous dinner. Through the closed door to the makeshift bedroom, she could hear Angelina opening and closing file drawers, then a loud bang. What on earth was the woman up to?

"Why didn't you go up?"

"To Robby's room last night?"

"Yeah."

Shrugging and coiling the phone cord around her fingers,

Ellie seated herself on the foldout couch. Somehow, it seemed impossible that, only a few hours ago, she and Robby had been making love right here. Unwanted physical sensations claimed her—heat and dampness, shivers and shudders. She recalled the playing piano music and the dim light, but mostly the greedy, insistent touch of his hands. Suddenly, she blinked. "What?"

"I said, if you followed him all the way to the hotel, why didn't you just go up?"

Sighing, Ellie pictured her friend. No doubt she was as gorgeous as ever, especially now that she and J.D. had made up and she was so happy in her marriage. "I don't know..." Her voice trailed off. "I guess I just felt confused. Nothing was going to come of it. Anyway, it's hard not to feel jealous of the relationship you've got with J.D. now."

"You know it hasn't always been this way."

The two had fought like cats and dogs, and for a long time, when J.D. was partying with his big-city friends, Susannah had done just about everything she could to avoid her own husband. "Maybe. But you all were made for each other."

There was a long pause. Then Susannah said, "Look, I'm tired of playing games. To both you and Robby, I've pretended like you're doing fine without each other, but you're not."

"You have?"

"Of course. I keep saying whatever seems best to make you jealous or want to get back together. I admit it, I'm trying to play matchmaker, but it's not working. I don't know why. You've been in love with the guy since you were a kid, and he's in love with you, and—"

"Oh, no, he's not."

"Yes, he is. And since you started sleeping together, you're ten times more smitten."

There was some truth in it. "Oh, Susannah, for a few months, I thought everything was going to work out, and that Robby and I would wind up together, but now…"

"You might still," Susannah put in.

Ellie shook her head adamantly. "No way."

"Well, you said Percy Anders wasn't exactly what you expected…"

Sighing, Ellie didn't want to rehash her date with the man once more. She was just about to respond when she heard a crash from the next room. Staring toward the closed door, she wondered what on earth her assistant was doing. "I'd better go." She paused. "By the way, when are you coming to town again?"

"In a few weeks. I've been keeping in touch with the manager at the restaurant every day, and it sounds like things are going well." When Susannah laughed, Ellie couldn't help but note the happy, self-satisfied quality in her voice. "It's amazing to think I'm making money when I'm not even there, but I miss working."

"If I didn't work, I wouldn't know what to do with myself," Ellie admitted. For so many years, Lee Polls had been the focus of her life, and lately she'd concentrated entirely on Future Trends, rarely going out for entertainment. She was good at what she did, yes, but as much as she hated to admit it, she could see where her father was coming from. Deep down, she knew he was desperate to have grandkids. Her mom, too. And her ne'er-do-well brothers probably weren't going to provide bundles of joy anytime soon. Ellie sighed once more. "I'd really better go," she said.

"I'll let you know…" Susannah's voice trailed off, and when she heard kissing noises, Ellie realized why and grinned. "Sounds like J.D. just came in."

Susannah giggled. "Yeah. He did."

"Hey there, Ellie," J.D. called out.

It was good to hear his voice, and Ellie's heart stretched to breaking. Susannah and J.D. could go to all their old haunts, such as Delia's or the Night Rider, while Ellie was stuck here. Of course, there were countless entertainment venues in the city, but nothing had the allure of home. "Let me know when you'll be in town," she managed to say, her voice catching with emotion. "I'll make up a bed."

Still sitting on the one she and Robby had used, she hung up the phone, feeling a strange mixture of pique and heartbreak. Robby's being here the previous night felt like a dream. Trying to push aside the thoughts as she rose, she strode to the door and opened it—only to interrupt another kiss.

Angelina's boyfriend, Antonio, stepped quickly backward, but not in time to hide just how hot the kiss had been. Angelina giggled nervously, quickly swiping her damp-looking mouth with the back of her hand. Her free hand flew to her hair, the French twist having almost come undone. She withdrew a hairpin, then stuck it back into a tangled mess of curls.

"Antonio was just leaving," she assured her breathlessly, smoothing the gray skirt of her suit, then grasping the hem of the jacket. Pulling it downward to straighten it.

Looking sheepish, the young man shoved a hand through his tousled black hair, then fished in his jeans pocket as if looking for something. "I was just on my way out."

Ellie couldn't help but chuckle. "Don't let me interrupt."

Sounding relieved, Antonio laughed. "I can't keep my hands off my bride-to-be."

Angelina lifted a hand, waving. "Bye, sweetie. I've got to work."

"I thought you'd be ready to grab a bite."

"One more hour, then we can eat."

"You can go now if you want," Ellie assured her.

"An hour," Angelina said firmly. "Antonio's been working night shifts, so he came downtown just to bother me."

Her fiancé merely laughed. "You love it."

"Maybe, but I want to finish a few things before lunch, and I'm not really hungry yet."

Her fiancé looked at his watch. "I'll wander around, then come back in an hour."

A moment later, he was out the door and Angelina smiled. "Seems like you were pretty busy last night, yourself."

Ellie squinted. "Huh?"

Grinning lustily, Angelina pulled open a desk drawer. When she peeked inside, Ellie blushed. Her panties were crumpled in the drawer. "Where were those?"

Laughing, Angelina nodded toward a spot near the bedroom door.

Ellie quickly shut the desk drawer. "Antonio didn't see them, did he?"

"No."

"I wonder how they got over there? Thank God nobody else saw them!" Ellie was fairly certain the heat in her cheeks was turning them scarlet. She couldn't help but remember Robby removing her underclothes. How could he have thrown the panties that far? Or...maybe they'd caught on her shoe as she was chasing him out of the house the previous night. Yes, that's probably what had happened. Shortly after she'd returned to the apartment, she'd gone to bed, hardly interested in cleaning the living room, but she was sure she'd picked up all the stray clothes.

"Whoops," she whispered.

Angelina laughed harder. "I put the cocktail glasses in the dishwasher."

Ellie winced. "I forgot about those, too."

"So things worked out with Percy." Angelina enthused. "I

knew it would! You worked so hard on collecting the data. When you first explained what you were trying to do, I *was* a little dubious."

Ellie could only stare. Did Angelina really think she'd slept with Percy? Should she tell her otherwise? "You were?"

Angelina nodded. "Antonio and I talked about it. I mean, we feel that love is natural, you know what I mean?"

It had sure felt that way the previous night. Chemistry had taken over, and the next thing Ellie had known, her clothes were being removed and Robby was carrying her to the bedroom. "Uh…I think I do."

"So it just seemed kind of weird to conduct a statistical analysis in order to find your dream man. At least that's what Antonio and I thought."

"You did?"

She nodded. "Yeah. But now, I'm thrilled it's worked out so well. Tell me all about it. Every single detail."

Ellie wasn't sure she wanted to share, especially not when Angelina really thought she'd been with Percy Anders all night. She shuddered at the thought, then felt a rush of guilt, since Percy had been well-mannered, at least. He wasn't a bad person, just unappealing to her. He was just a little too needy…or something. Ellie couldn't quite put a finger on what was wrong.

Percy was so different from Robby, the polar opposite. Noticing her gaze had fixed on the traffic outside, she startled. She could swear she'd just glimpsed a dark sedan outside. By the time she registered it, it had driven past already, but she could swear she'd seen the two men from the previous night. Or was it just her imagination? There were many such cars in New York, of course, but maybe it had been following Robby, after all. Her gut was telling her that it was the truth, even if she could think of no good reason for it.

Suddenly, she gasped out loud. A while back, Susannah had said Charlie was getting out of prison. Maybe his release was somehow connected to the appearance of these men.

"What?" Ellie asked, realizing Angelina had spoken.

"When's your next date?"

For a moment, Ellie could scarcely remember what the two had been talking about. Maybe she should close the office when Angelina left for lunch and return to the hotel to see if Robby was still there. She dreaded seeing him, of course. At least that's what she told herself, but if there was something wrong and she hadn't warned him…well, she'd never be able to live with herself.

"When?" Angelina prodded.

"Soon," Ellie assured her, now heaving a sigh, wondering how on earth she'd be able to endure another date with Percy.

"Good," gushed Angelina. "You were on another phone line in the next room, but that guy called from the newspaper, and I—"

"Derrick Mills?"

"Yes, that's his name."

With a sinking heart, Ellie said, "And you what?"

"I told him that from the looks of the place this morning, you and Percy Anders had a really good time last night."

Ellie's lips parted in astonishment. "You didn't?"

"I did." Angelina gave her arm a squeeze. "Oh, I didn't go into all the details. I mean, about the panties and cocktail glasses you left out."

"Well…thank you for that," Ellie muttered. Thankfully, the newspaper wasn't a tabloid, so the gossip wouldn't be on the front page tomorrow.

"I'm happy for you," Angelina blurted. "Between the lines, it's clear you had some sort of bad breakup, so I'm doubly glad."

Ellie thought of Robby again, then the black sedan. She could swear she'd seen the same two men drive by, but it was sunny outside and the windows of the car were reflecting glare. Was she looking for an excuse to go to Robby? Or should she try to warn him just in case?

"C'mon, let's get started planning your next date with Percy," Angelina was saying. "I'm sure Derrick Mills will be thrilled to hear something's on the burner. I said you or I would call as soon as something is set up…" Suddenly, she glanced at Ellie. "Or maybe you'd rather be alone this time and not let any newspapers know. I know this is sort of a publicity stunt, but still, your relationship should be the most important thing."

"Let me think about it," Ellie murmured, but her mind was fixed on Robby, and whether or not something was wrong.

9

SIGHING WHEN HE HEARD a knock on the door, Robby glanced at a bedside clock. Technically, an hour remained before he had to leave the hotel, but he figured the visitor might be a maid, checking to see if he'd gone, so she could clean.

"Give me another minute." Lowering his voice, he muttered to himself, "I should have left before now." There had been no direct flights the previous night, however, so he'd settled on catching a plane later this afternoon.

Otherwise, he'd put off traveling for the wrong reasons. He hated to acknowledge it, but he'd been tempted to return to Ellie's apartment. He'd been toying with the idea for hours. Dammit, he was usually so cool, calm and collected, but making love with Ellie had twisted his thoughts into knots, as usual. Decisive by nature, he seemed to lose his inner compass and sense of direction every time he touched her.

"Don't let her make you crazy again," he said, coaching himself. Over the past months, he'd finally managed to get his head screwed on straight. Often, he'd forgotten about Ellie for hours at a time, at least until Daddy Eddie started talking about her. If Robby hadn't known better, he'd have thought Daddy Eddie was intentionally trying to torture him.

Even without Daddy Eddie's constant harangue, Robby couldn't let go of his thoughts today. Her image was burned into his retina after last night, the picture of her fixed permanently to his mind's eye. Her sweet taste had clung to his lips and her heady scent to his skin, although he'd taken a cold shower immediately, to wash away whatever might prompt recollections. He'd watched TV, too, hoping to distract himself, but it hadn't helped, then he'd tossed and turned all night.

Now, he wished he could think of one good reason to return to Banner. He didn't feel like working. Not that he minded the problems Ellie was causing—he liked a good challenge—but Lee Polls always reminded him of her, especially her empty office, which was right across the hallway. Every time he looked up from his work, he'd find himself staring at her desk.

Anyway, with his luck, as soon as he got back to town, he'd run into Charlie. He glanced toward the door. Since no second knock had followed the first, no doubt the maid had found another room to clean. Taking a deep breath, Robby took a final look around, making sure he'd gathered all his belongings. Shouldering his duffel, he reached into his pocket, then left a tip on the night table.

Was he really leaving New York without seeing Ellie again? "Yeah," he muttered to himself. He was. And after that, he'd never look back. Maybe he'd see her at some work-related trade show someday….

Or maybe not. Future Trends was a viable company, and yet Ellie had turned down the possibility of a merger. If nothing else, her acceptance of a deal would have bridged their separate worlds. It would have been a way of saying she was still interested. "And she's got a man, anyway."

Another knock sounded.

Maybe the maid hadn't found another vacant room, after all. "Coming," he called once more, then he strode purposefully to the door and opened it.

"Robby." There was a long, awkward pause. She added, "Uh…hello."

"Ellie," he managed to say, her name leaving his lungs in a whooshing breath. Inadvertently, he stepped backward. "I wasn't expecting you."

"I guess you weren't."

It was an understatement. "Well…hello," he said again.

She came forward a few steps, as if impelled by an unseen force, and as she crossed the threshold, the door swung shut, moving on its own momentum. All at once, everything seemed remarkably quiet. From far off, through the closed windows, he could hear muted sounds from the traffic below.

Closer, Ellie's breath was a soft pant, making him think she could have run all the way here, although she hadn't, obviously. Still, her dark hair looked windblown and was gleaming with touches of sun, her blue eyes were sparkling, and her cheeks were all peaches-and-cream. They were flushed, the pink color deepening by the second as if she were a little embarrassed, although Robby couldn't fathom what could make her feel that way.

He was the one who should be embarrassed, he thought. He, not she, had come all the way here from Banner to see her. His lips parted, and he started to speak, then he thought the better of it. What he was thinking was none of her damn business, after all. Still, she looked like a million bucks. Beneath an open, casual tan coat, she wore a dark brown chocolate skirt and matching striped brown-and-tan jacket, brown hose and high-heeled shoes. She may have been dressed for work, but despite the primness of the attire—or maybe because of it—he felt an unwanted surge of desire. Not to mention a little scruffy, himself, since he was wearing worn jeans and a dark, long-sleeved pullover shirt.

"I'm sorry to bother you," she began.

"No bother," he found himself saying. Immediately, he wanted to kick himself because he'd spoken too fast, leaving the impression that he'd drop everything if the damn woman decided to waltz back into his life. What did she think he was—some toy dog who'd spin around, wag his tail and do parlor tricks anytime she entered a room or threw him a bone?

And yet, his chest had gotten tight with anticipation, his heart beating too hard and fast. Why had she come?

"You really do look like you're on your way out," she said.

He nodded without commitment. She seemed tired, not that the effects of a sleepless night stopped him from experiencing another age-old pang at his groin. He had no idea why Ellie always affected him this way. She was the prettiest girl in the world, but if the truth be told, surely, every other man would think his own lady was just as attractive.

From the second he'd opened the door, though, his blood had charged with electricity. It was as if he'd been plugged into a light socket. As the current leaped and danced through his veins, he had to fight not to shudder. *Careful, or you're going to have a replay of last night,* he coached himself.

Nevertheless, before he thought it through, he was lowering his duffel to the floor so he could take a better look at her, feeling strangely elated once more when he noted the dark circles beneath her eyes. She really hadn't slept any better than he. Despite that, she was every bit as sexy as she had been the previous night, and somehow, it was comforting to know that he wasn't the only one affected by what had happened at her apartment.

"You're heading out to catch a flight?"

"I've got a minute."

"I have something to tell you."

"No problem."

Yes, he really could have kicked himself for the accommodating tone. Just because she had decided to track him to his hotel today didn't mean he had to make time for her. As his eyes drifted over her, moving from her rose-tinged cheeks to the crisp white blouse under her suit jacket, he felt every bit as powerless as he had the night before. He just wished he had some control over his involuntary reactions, but his pulse was skyrocketing, his breath quickening, and the hairs at the nape of his neck tingling.

Taking a deep breath, he dragged splayed fingers through his hair, absently ruffling the dark strands, then not quite knowing what to do with himself, he shoved the same hand deeply into his pants pocket. "You wanted to tell me something?"

"Yes. It was about last night…"

Maybe, but her gaze seemed fixated on his mouth. Maybe she, too, was remembering the kisses they'd shared. No doubt that's why she'd come. He stepped toward her as if drawn by a magnet, and she stepped back, almost in tandem, seeming to sense his intentions. Her back landed against the closed door, and the next thing he knew his finger was on her lips as if to silence her.

"I'm glad you came," he murmured.

Something flinty caught in her blue-eyed gaze, an emotion that was hard to interpret—woundedness and distrust, maybe. "You are?"

She'd said it as if she didn't believe him, which only made him want to wreathe his arms around her neck once more. As usual, she was twisting him into knots. "Yeah."

"After the way you left me last night?"

"Dammit, Ellie," he muttered, softly cursing and wondering what she'd expected him to do. Stepping even closer to cover the fraction of space remaining between them, he reached to touch her, then realized his gesture might not be welcome. He wound up placing his hand just above her head.

Since she was wearing high heels, she was almost as tall as he, and so he was near enough to feel her breath on his face now. For a moment, he looked deeply into her eyes. They were breathtakingly blue, even more so than he'd remembered. The irises were the color of the sky over the ocean on a clear day, and the pupils bright, shiny dots of black.

Those gorgeous eyes were penetrating his. "What?" she asked.

He'd almost forgotten what he was going to say. "I couldn't stay last night," he finally muttered, his hand now dropping to her shoulder, his fingers curling downward toward her upper arm, offering the faintest hint of a massage. "I had to leave. I figured you'd understand."

"Understand what? That you had to scratch an itch?" she accused, her voice tense. "Wham, bam, thank you, ma'am?"

His lips parted in surprise. "You know better than that."

"Do I?"

"It was you who left me." Was she really going to try to turn the situation around?

"In Banner?"

"Where else?"

"I didn't have a choice, not after what you did to me."

He wasn't going to rehash that argument. "Be that as it may, you left me, not the other way around. And when I came to your place last night, I didn't mean for us to…"

"Have sex?"

He nodded.

"But you did, anyway?"

"You did, too."

"I didn't initiate it."

Same old Ellie. "The dress was a provocation."

"I was already wearing it."

"For your date."

Her eyes tested him. "What of it?"

His jaw set. "Nothing. I can tell you've…moved on. That's why I took off last night."

"Not before you…"

"How could I help myself?" he whispered now, not bothering to argue with her last point, his hand dropping another fraction, the heel of his palm near the rising mound of her breast. "How could I, Ellie?" he repeated, shocked to hear the broken quality of his voice.

"You could have done what you came to my apartment to do."

"I did."

"No, the other thing."

He had no idea what she was talking about. His gaze had landed on her mouth, and he was exploring the contours of her lips. They looked as soft as he knew they felt, her teeth white, shiny and inviting. He just wished she was smiling, but instead, a pout had claimed her mouth. "What I came to do?"

"Offering me Daddy's deal."

His throat tightened. The deal was real enough, although he'd desperately wanted to see Ellie. "Well, you didn't take me up on the offer." Which meant she was ending things and never wanted an excuse to see him again.

For a long moment, they just stared at each other. Robby was aware of the ache at his groin, now it was almost painful. Dammit, he felt like a hand had reached out and grabbed him, fondling and teasing, cupping and massaging—and all the while, a voice in his ear was telling him that she'd never stick around to satisfy him again. Every fiber of his being wanted to draw her into a tight embrace. He didn't want to let her go….

He felt as if he'd pop like a cork. Frustrations had bottled up inside him, and only a genie named Ellie could set them free. Yes, he was like a lamp that needed rubbing, and only her magic could cure what ailed him. Instinctively, he knew she was feeling the power of their attraction, too. She didn't want to feel it, but the force was undeniable.

Just from looking at her, he was tingling all over. His other hand found her shoulder, then both traveled down the lengths of her arms. When they reached her elbows, he transferred the touch to her waist, nestling it under her open jacket, loving how his fingers settled on her crisp white blouse, right in the nip of the curve.

His heart was hammering hard, and the pang at his groin nearly brought him to his knees. His hands lowered yet again, now molding slowly over the curves of her hips. Beneath his palms, the fabric of her skirt felt coarse, making him long to feel her stockings, which were probably silk, or better yet, her smooth, milky bare skin. Under his fly, he became uncomfortably aware of how tight he felt, engorging, lengthening, getting ready….

It had happened that quickly. A second ago, they'd been arguing. Now, he was caressing her hips and she wasn't stopping him.

"We can't…" she whispered.

She didn't sound convinced. His eyes never left hers. Blue on blue, steady and searing with need. "Watch me," he whispered back.

He could see her throat work as she swallowed, how her tongue darted out to lick her lips, seemingly against their dryness. This was what she'd come for, after all. He knew it. And she knew it. Just like that, as quickly as a heartbeat, he'd gotten hard for her, and no doubt, she was wet for him.

Ever so slowly, he leaned a fraction so his fingers could catch the hem of the skirt and lift it. Rustling his hands beneath, he found the waistband of her panty hose and quickly tugged them down to her upper thighs, so the gauzy fabric was trapping her legs, keeping them pressed together.

She uttered a soft sound of compliance, parting for him, despite the confining hose. Being trapped like that just seemed to make her hotter, and he thrust his hand down, arrowing his fingers through her tangled, moist pubic hair. He was inside her panties quickly, his fingers exploring, then thrusting upward, driving deeply inside her. His mouth covered hers, stifling any protest. Not that she would, judging from the immediate response; the velvet-hot spear of her tongue tussled and played, demanding his.

Groaning against her lips, then parting them farther with his tongue, he sparred back, licking, vibrating, sweeping the interior of her mouth and toying with her teeth. Between her legs, she was sweet and soft, the skin of her thighs as soft as water, her sex dripping as her hungry hands sought him, fondling him through his jeans. At just the merest touch, he thought he'd explode.

Without breaking the kiss, he headed to the bed by backing up and pulling her along with him. And then everything seemed to happen at once. His knees hit the back of the mattress, curled over it, and he landed on his back with her falling on top of him, stumbling because of how the hose, only half removed, had constricted her.

By the time the kiss broke, they were hot and panting. She was shrugging out of her overcoat and the jacket that went with her suit. Somehow, he pulled his shirt over his head and tossed it aside, then thrust both his hands into her hair. Moaning, he simply couldn't believe the softness of the strands as gorgeous silk spun and tumbled through his fingers.

Meantime, she was shimmying and shaking on top of him, creaming and gushing and driving him crazy with lust as she wiggled out of hose and panties, her every movement near his crotch a promise of what was to come. He was powerless but to writhe beneath her, his hands leaving her soft hair and gripping her hips, his fingers now sinking into the silken flesh just below her tiny waist, wanting nothing more than to bring her whole weight down upon him.

That, he realized now, or to see her breasts… His temperature spiked, sending coils of heat through his body, since she seemed to read his mind. She was perched above him, her bare knees bracketing his thighs, the hot, sweet core of her poised right above where he was so painfully hard, still gloved by denim, which was stretching uncomfortably. Quickly, her fingers shaking as if she couldn't undress herself fast enough, she undid the buttons of her blouse.

What he saw as the white shirttails parted made him moan out loud with raw need. The sound was almost foreign to his own ears, coming from somewhere deep in his chest, then sticking way down in his throat. It seemed to reverberate in his groin, which throbbed in exact tandem. What a vision. Her breasts were cresting right over the rim of a chaste white lace bra, spilling over the cups for his eyes, begging for his hands, swaying slightly with her movements. Her skin was pure peachy cream, the half-moons of lace barely hiding the dark, perky, aroused buds of her nipples.

She didn't bother with her skirt, just pushed it upward, around her waist. She was so hot that she didn't care if her clothes got wrinkled. Reaching between their bodies, he unbuckled his belt, his eyes still fixed on her sloping breasts. "Take your bra off," he commanded, his voice husky, almost guttural. "Let me see you, baby."

Her fingers slid into the ample cleavage. She found a front catch, then slowly released it. Taking her time, she separated the cups, opening them until he could see all of her. She pushed the lace fabric to the side. His hand was still on his belt. Now he pushed his jeans and briefs downward. As he arched and lifted his hips, so he could drag his clothes at least to his knees, he gasped. Even soft cotton seemed to chaff his burning erection.

He came free, hard and throbbing. Her hand reached between them and she grasped him, making his mouth go bone-dry. His head veered back and his eyes slammed shut. As she fisted him, sliding her hand along his length, he couldn't believe how good her touch felt. He just wished he wasn't somewhat trapped by his confining clothing, the jeans stretching across his thighs, but she wasn't going to give him time to finish undressing.

Already, she let go of him, and now she was scooting closer, to guide him inside her. She stopped just shy of him, leaving him in torture. He was arching…straining and aching, the head of his penis begging for the curative salve of her drenching heat. Lifting his hips higher, he urged her nearer, so she could slide down on the hot length.

Instead, she merely swung her hips, brushing over him… back and forth. Her knees squeezed him. Her moist curls tickling him, she let the exposed head part her, opening her lower lips, then settle at the entrance. She lowered herself ever so slowly then, just an inch, then another, until he uttered a string of harsh male sounds that were either curses or pleas, he wasn't sure which.

Raising his hands, he molded them over her breasts. They were hanging low, close to his mouth, and although he could capture a bud with ease, he didn't. Instead, he just surveyed the luscious fruit, the handfuls of milk-and-honey, the vision of sweet skin.

"Does that feel good?" she whispered.

Gritting his teeth, he felt her slide downward another blessed inch, so his engorged length was stretching her more, and he sucked in a sizzling breath. Reaching like a kid in a candy store, he gently pinched the tips of her breasts, loving how the nipples hardened, turning darker red, almost the color of wine.

She drew an audible breath, so he plucked some more, picking the sweet fruit, making her whimper. Pressing his fingers absently into his mouth, he dampened them from between his lips, then applied the wetness directly to her nipples. Grasping the dampened, tightened buds, he tugged them, further distending them…

She started panting hard and he suddenly thrust, lifting his hips, demanding her to take more. "Yes," he whispered, feeling her stretch.

"You feel so big," she rasped. "So hard."

He was. And she was slick, wrapping around him like a hot, wet glove. Her plea broke the silence, then a frustrated whimper as he once more coated his fingers with saliva and drenched her nipples. Blowing where they were so wet, he watched them strain. He wanted to grasp her hips then…to settle his huge hands there and force her hips downward, until she was riding him hard. He was about to explode.

"Oh, yeah," he suddenly whispered senselessly, as she began moving in earnest. His hands dropped from her breasts to bracket her ribs. Her wild breaths made her chest rise and fall rapidly, and her thighs felt weak, shaking against his, the flesh quivering. Scalding hot, she lowered herself again and again, and he touched her belly, then lower.

She was trembling all over, sinking all the way down, onto his length, until he was buried to the hilt. She creamed even more when he reached between them and grasped her wet lower curls in a fistful. Settling the pad of his thumb on the bud of her clitoris, he let it slip and slide. Her head tilted back. She looked glorious now, riding him, thrusting her pelvis, the wild, spiced scent of her pungent.

Somehow, he held on to his control, his mouth blistering and dry now, his eyes captivated by her swaying breasts, the dark tight tips still making obvious how hot she felt. Over and over, she thrust her pelvis, demanding that his thumb massage her clitoris deeply. Then she'd drop her whole weight downward, taking his whole burning length. He felt himself surge upward, encased in liquid fire milking each inch of him. She came upward, slower now, reveling in pure needy fire, only to thrust her pelvis toward his thumb once more, so he could caress…press…circle…

"Slip and slide," he whispered as the thumb did its magic. She cried out, then swiftly came down once more, riding him hard, filling herself completely with his hard, hot length. Cocked and ready, his release right there…a second away…a breath…

But she wasn't coming. He wanted to wait, yet it was all too much. The silken brush of her watery thighs against his coarser, hairy legs was doing him in. So were her breasts, swinging faster and lower, coming nearer to his lips as her movements became less voluntary. He tried to brace himself by opening his legs more, having forgotten his knees were trapped by the jeans.

Groaning in crazed frustration, he tried to stave off release. But he wanted it badly. He felt he'd beg, borrow, cheat or steal if he could get it. Anything. He just wanted it to end.

Breathing hard, he clasped his arms, tucking them beneath his head. He made himself fully open to her, with his back arched, his belly taut. "Ride me," he urged her.

The light from the window dancing on her skin as he forced himself to remain still. "C'mon, baby," his voice strangled. "Let me see you do all the work."

She was getting hot and sweaty now, taking her pleasure just the way she wanted. She was so brazen, totally shameless, completely in control. She knew exactly how she wanted her man…and she was taking him. All his energy was starting to focus between his legs. In just a minute, he was going to lose control and…

Her hands were planted on his chest, the palms deliciously damp, the fingertips digging into his skin. They hadn't yet kissed again, and he didn't want that. Instead, he wanted to study her facial expression as she lost control.

And yet he had to touch her again. Just her swaying breasts. Wetting his fingers once more, sloppily this time, he lathered the nipples with saliva, and she sobbed at the touch. Greedily, he grasped at them. Her fingers curled on his pectorals, clutching. His responded, folding over her dampened breasts, to knead and squeeze. She was going for her orgasm now, so his touch held no gentleness or reserve or pity. He pinched, rolled, teased…

Suddenly, he got completely rigid inside her. His knees veered up and he rocked her, his upper thighs creating a cradle for her backside. Groaning, he almost lost control himself now…coming so close…until they were both moaning, groaning, writhing and hot with sweat. "You're with me…be with me…" she cried.

She leaned forward, crouching; the nipples he'd dampened brushed his nipples, feeling like a match to kindling in dry heat. A brush fire roared through him as her breasts continued sweeping his chest, teasing the coarse hair coating his muscles.

"Kiss me," he whispered.

Their tongues met. Not their mouths and lips, just their tongues—distended, wet, straining, greedy.

"You got me," she breathed. It was something she often said right before she came.

"And you got me," he echoed her as he convulsed. Shutting his eyes, he spilled inside her, and he gasped as he felt her gushing. Both his arms circled her, and he hugged her tightly, curling his face into her shoulder as the tight pulsing palpitations of her body milked him dry.

And after a long time, he gently brushed the hair away from her face and kissed her slowly, offering a deep, openmouthed kiss that seemed to last forever. Leaning back a fraction, just enough to see her face, he roved his gaze over it as if he might never see her again.

She smiled.

He smiled back. Hers was one of those truly female smiles, he decided. It was mysterious and all knowing. "You've got a smile like the Mona Lisa," he whispered.

"You make me smile."

"Why's that?"

"You're sexy."

He smiled. "You think?"

"Fishing for compliments?"

"Sure."

"Well…you're built like a house," she said.

He was still inside her, his desire. "Not anymore," he offered with a soft chuckle.

"I don't think I could take any more," she assured him.

"Maybe not now."

They had things to work out, to be sure, but after lovemaking such as this, surely some solution could be reached. He was just about to broach the subject when loud music blared. Startling, she quickly relaxed and said, "My phone."

"Cell?"

She nodded. He moaned as she quickly got up; the separation of their bodies made him feel utterly bereft. "Oh, no," he muttered playfully, offering her a bad-boy pout.

"You'll get over it," she said, digging into her coat pocket, finding the phone.

"I doubt it," he countered, his eyes flickering over her. The skirt was still pushed around her waist, and her blouse and bra were open. "You look awful good."

She pressed the phone's talk button while still eyeing him, her gorgeous blue eyes sparkling. "Hello?"

In that moment, she looked like the same old Ellie he

remembered, so confident and happy and successful, always ready for sex. It was the way he wanted her to feel all the time. Suddenly, he squinted, his eyes narrowing. Only then did he realize his attention had settled between her legs, on the lovely thatch of curly damp hair. He glanced up, frowning when he saw her alarmed expression.

"Robbed? Are you sure?" After a long pause, she continued, "Well, what happened exactly?" Another pause, then, "Did you already call the police?" Her eyes widening, she shook her head. "I'm on my way. Just tell them everything when they're there."

Disconnecting, she looked at him. "My office was robbed."

He was sitting up, pulling up his pants. "What?"

"Robbed," she repeated.

Grabbing his shirt, he shrugged into it. "What did they take?"

She shook her head, smoothing her skirt. "I don't know. Maybe nothing. Angelina said the computers were there, but it looked as if the place had been ransacked. She went out to lunch for an hour. That's when I came here. When she got back, a window was open. Somebody climbed in and went through the files."

"What could they be looking for?"

"I don't know." Lifting her panties and hose from the floor, she put them on, then shoved her feet into her shoes.

"The file drawers were open."

"Information?"

"I don't know what," she repeated. "The data in those files is readily accessible anywhere else."

"Maybe the person, or people, didn't know that. Did she say how many?"

"She didn't see anyone. What could they be looking for?"

He considered. "I guess we'll see."

She glanced at him. "You don't need to…"

"I was just about to check out of the hotel," he said. "Of course I'll come with you." He hesitated, then decided not to tell her he had a flight. Who knew? Maybe he'd wind up staying another night.

Gasping, she brought a hand to her mouth as if to cover it. "That's why I came here," she said.

He circled both arms around her waist and drew her close, wishing like hell that they weren't dressed. Pressed against him, she felt warm and delicious. "I thought it was to have sex with me."

"No…" Her eyes turned a darker blue as they searched his. "I…"

Feeling alarmed, he prompted, "What, Ellie?" There was something, obviously, that she didn't want to tell him.

"Last night, I followed you here."

His heart filled, stretching to breaking. "You did? So it wasn't just today?"

She hesitated. "Yes. But it wasn't what you think."

"Which is?"

"That I just wanted to have sex." Pausing, she amended, "Well…maybe it was. I don't know. Anyway, when I left the apartment last night, I saw two men in a dark sedan outside. I didn't think much of it, at least not until they headed in exactly the same direction of your cab and mine."

"What did the guys look like?"

She described them. "But it was dark," she added. "And I was preoccupied, to be honest. I didn't see them well, nor pay much attention at first. In fact, we lost them in traffic, but when we got here, your cab went through a light and I had to wait.

"Meanwhile, the two guys pulled in behind you and raced in, almost as if to catch up with you. When I reached the hotel, they were just leaving. I asked the clerk if they were checked in, but he said he couldn't give me information…" Her voice trailed off. "Anyway, I changed my mind about seeing you, and I decided that spotting those men was just a coincidence or my mind playing tricks. Then this morning, I changed my mind again, and thought maybe you should know, just in case something was afoot, in case…"

He was worried for her safety, and the gears in his mind were spinning a million miles a minute. "What?"

"In case those men really were asking about you. I thought maybe it had to do with Charlie. I hate to bring him up," she hastily said, "but Susannah says your dad is due to get out of prison—"

"That bastard!" he exploded, his whole body seized by emotion. The man hadn't been out of jail but a few days and already he was destroying Robby's life again. What had he done this time? And, dammit, it didn't help that he'd really thought Ellie had come only to make love to him. But, no…that had only been an afterthought. "If my old man's done anything that's endangered you, somehow, I'll kill him," Robby muttered.

"Calm down," she whispered.

"Hell, no, I'm not calming down." Instead, he turned toward the bedside table and picked up a phone. It took three calls to track Charlie at Hodges Motor Lodge, but only when his father answered did Robby realize how unprepared he was to hear his father's voice.

"Hello?"

Robby hesitated, fighting the impulse to simply hang up. Besides, he didn't know whether to call the man "Dad" or "Charlie." Neither felt right. "This is Robby," he began.

"Robby!" Charlie exclaimed immediately, his voice packed with emotion. "I was hoping you'd call me, son. I've thought about you. You wouldn't believe how much. I—"

"This is just a quick call," Robby interjected tersely. "I want to know if you're in some kind of trouble already."

"Trouble? No...of course not. What would make you think that?"

At least he sounded sober. "I'm in New York and Ellie Lee's here. She says she saw two guys in a dark sedan follow me last night. Today she got robbed. Seeing as she and I live honestly within the law, and that you're the only person I know who doesn't, I figured you might know something."

There was a long pause, then Charlie said, "Oh, my God. No...that's impossible."

Robby's voice sharpened, since it sounded as if his father might know something. "Why impossible?"

"I don't know," his father muttered.

But it sounded like a lie. "If something happens to Ellie," Robby began.

"Nothing is going to happen to her," Charlie said. "I haven't done anything, either."

The man seemed so sincere Robby could almost imagine he didn't. But then, his father had never seemed truly responsible for the death of Shirley Fey. "Well, if you think of something, get in touch with me. I'm in New York now, but I'll be home soon. I'm in the book. You can leave a message."

"I didn't do anything," Charlie repeated.

"Well, then," returned Robby. "That's the only reason I called, and all I needed to know."

With that, he hung up. When he turned to face Ellie, he was surprised to find that she was so close. Stepping right into his arms, she asked, "Are you okay?"

Nodding, he wrapped his arms around her waist and pulled her close. Angling his head downward, he swept his lips across hers. "I'm fine."

"I know you didn't want to talk to him."

"Actually, I feel relieved in a way. At least some of the

dread about hearing his voice is gone. I don't think it'll be so hard when I see him face-to-face, which I'm bound to do."

"Maybe he's changed."

"Doubtful." Leaning his head a fraction, Robby kissed her once more, pressing his lips firmly to hers. "We'd better get to your place," he murmured.

"I'd rather make love again."

"Me, too."

A knock sounded at the door, startling them both. "Maid service," a woman called.

So there she was. "We're on our way out," Robby called.

"Not before you kiss me one more time," Ellie demanded.

Right before his mouth covered hers again, he responded, "My pleasure."

And then, after the kiss, he grabbed her hand and headed for the door. "I just hope my father's not to blame for whatever's going on."

"Why?"

"Just because," he muttered tersely. But if Ellie Lee was ever harmed, Robby Robriquet would make sure there'd be hell to pay.

10

"TAKE ANOTHER GOOD look around and make sure nothing's missing, ma'am." The cop sent by the precinct was a tall, blond looker named Lief Hoffman. He was big and solid, built like a house. His shoulders stretched the seams of his blue uniform shirt to bursting, and his slacks looked as though they could scarcely contain his bulging thighs.

"I'm sure nothing's gone," Ellie said, glad when she registered Robby's supportive hand on her back. Funny, she thought now, how such a small gesture could make her feel so comforted. His body moved easily with hers, both in bed and out of it, something that had always made her feel sure they were meant to be together.

Although the space that served as both her office and apartment had been vandalized, she did feel safe now with Robby by her side. As soon as they'd made love, she'd felt a sense of well-being for the first time in months. Maybe she could even reconcile with her father someday, she now thought with a surge of hope, although she couldn't foresee how. Still thinking of the separation, she felt her heart squeeze with pain. How had her life gone so awry? Should she have simply accepted the situation when Daddy Eddie promoted Robby? Should she have stayed?

No...Lee Polls had been such a large part of her life. Shaking her head, she reprimanded herself for getting soft.

Robby's sweet lovemaking had been wonderful, but it was to blame for her muddled thinking. That or the cab ride to her apartment, during which Robby had threaded his fingers through hers, resting her hand gently on his thigh.

No matter how good it felt, he and Daddy Eddie had played her for a fool, and she'd better not forget it. Nevertheless, even now, an undeniable thrill shot through her system, when she thought of how worried Robby had sounded about her safety. If anything bad happened to her, he'd retaliate.

Of course, his protective attitude might have more to do with his anger at Charlie than his love for her, she told herself, feeling bad about the rift between Robby and his dad. Many people around Banner, including Daddy Eddie, had long viewed Charlie as more weak than malicious, after all.

Whatever the case, the man's flaws had deadly effects for Shirley Fey, so Ellie understood the reasons for Robby's cold fury. Her heart squeezed with pain once more. Daddy Eddie could hardly be compared to Charlie, but he'd done something unforgivable, just the same. Would she find some way to forgive him? Or would the break in relationship haunt her for the rest of her life? Would her anger persist for years just as Robby's?

"Are you positive the guy didn't take anything?" Officer Hoffman repeated.

"Yes, take another look, Ellie," Robby urged.

Since Angelina had left the window open, allowing the intruder to enter, the officer's colleagues, now outside, had dusted the area for fingerprints. A fine powder coated all the surfaces. When she surveyed the open drawers to the file cabinets, she felt disheartened. Folders were strewn across the floor; papers were everywhere.

How could this be happening? It was nearly as strange as the fact that Robby Robriquet was with her in New York. "Whoever broke in really did make a mess. I don't think I need to check the other room again. I'm sure nothing's gone." She groaned. "But why would somebody do this? Just to be destructive? It doesn't make any sense."

"Should I start cleaning?" Angelina asked, casting an inquiring glance at Officer Hoffman.

"I'm not working," put in Antonio. "So I can help. I don't mind."

"That's nice of you to offer," Ellie said, impressed. Antonio was obviously smitten, and whenever Ellie saw him, he was busy trying to steal an intimate sensual moment with his fiancée. Now it seemed clear there was more to the young man than met the eye. He was in his early twenties, with liquid jet eyes and dark hair, a long lock of which fell across his forehead, curling like a question mark. "I mean it," he repeated. "I'd be glad to do whatever I can."

"And I can stay late tonight," offered Angelina.

"You two are the best," said Ellie. And yet when she glanced at the lovebirds, she did a quick double take. Was it her imagination or had they exchanged a significant look. Were they hiding something from her? Had they withheld some sort of information? But, no…that was crazy. Angelina and Antonio were nice people. "What?" she asked in response to her gut, her eyebrows knitting in question.

"Nothing," Angelina replied quickly. Then she added, "I feel like this whole thing is my fault."

It wasn't the first time she'd said that since Ellie and Robby had arrived. "Don't be silly," Ellie told her.

"Yeah, don't be so hard on yourself," Robby echoed.

Angelina insisted, "I'm the one who opened the window earlier. The heat came on…and, well, you know how that old steam radiator works? It's always either freezing or boiling in here. So, after it came on, I opened the window for a minute to cool the place down. When I closed it, I guess I didn't relock it."

Officer Hoffman said, "Try to think back, visualize what you did."

"I'm sure I didn't," Angelina stated, looking positively stricken by her oversight as she began to lift file folders from the floor. "I'm so sorry. There's electronic backup for everything, but it's always nice when the papers are in their proper places."

Ellie's gaze meshed with Robby's and for a moment she couldn't think straight. His eyes were really something—a deep dark blue that made her think of oceans and warm cuddling near campfires. She wanted to grab his hand and leave, then find a place where she could snuggle against him. Yes, he'd come here only because her father had sent him. But maybe, after last night and today, his motives had changed.

She cut off her own thoughts. Dammit, what was wrong with her? Oh, she yearned for Robby, body and soul, but nothing had changed. She could accept him on his old terms, which wouldn't work, or on his new terms, which meant cow-towing to him and Daddy Eddie and accepting his business deal.

That would open the door to having a relationship again, but at what cost? It would never be the same as before, she decided, where they were like equal partners. She shook her head once more, to clear it of confusion. "The two guys," she said, snapping out of her reverie.

"Two guys?" Officer Hoffman interjected.

She nodded. "There were two outside last night…"

"Yes. Ellie…" Robby glanced away "…had a date last night, but I came over afterward."

"You did?" Angelina uttered a gasp, her eyes narrowing with understanding. "That explains the…"

"The what?" Officer Hoffman spoke again.

Her cheeks tinged pink, Angelina glanced between Robby and Ellie. "When I came in this morning, there were glasses out, so it was clear that company had been here, but I thought…"

"It was Percy Anders," Ellie finished.

"Your...first date?" Office Hoffman asked Ellie.

"That was his name." Ellie nodded, wondering what exactly to say, and feeling half pleased since Robby obviously wasn't thrilled about Percy. Not that the other man could hold a candle to Robby, but Robby never had to know that. Once more, she caught her own thoughts and censured them. She had to quit worrying about what Robby thought.

Officer Hoffman continued. "Wasn't there a story about you in the newspaper?"

"Yes. I conducted a poll... It was a sort of publicity stunt to find myself the right man."

"And this fellow, Percy Anders, turned out to be the one?"

"Yes. Last night was my first date with him."

"So how did the date go?"

Ellie hesitated. If she admitted her true feelings, she'd lose any leverage when it came to making Robby jealous. Once more, she could have kicked herself. The relationship was over. "Well, we went out to dinner. It was...civil."

"Civil?" Officer Hoffman frowned. "Did he seem...."

"Weird?" Ellie decided she'd better be honest. After all, this could be serious. "No. Definitely not like a stalker or anything like that. He was a little awkward with women. It didn't...seem like he dated much."

"I think you're barking up the wrong tree," Robby cut in, seeming less concerned about Percy than in other aspects of the break-in. "My father just got out of jail," he began. Speaking directly to the officer, he detailed the history of Charlie's legal troubles, beginning with his history as a town drunk and ending with the death of Shirley Fey and his recent release from jail. After that, Robby said, "So, last night, I came to see Ellie."

"After Percy Anders left?" asked the officer.

"He was still here." Robby flashed a quick glance at Ellie,

but his emotions were unreadable. "So I waited outside. Then I came in and…"

"And?"

"And…" Robby began.

"And he stayed a while," Ellie put in. "About…an hour, maybe longer, then he left."

"But she followed me."

Officer Hoffman was squinting harder. Angelina quit shuffling papers so she could listen, and Antonio seated himself in one of the chairs by the fireplace, as if just to watch the show.

Officer Hoffman said, "Did you two have a fight?"

"Sort of," replied Robby.

"You did or you didn't," Angelina commented.

Antonio nodded. "Fighting is not a mixed bag."

"We didn't really fight. I just had to leave," Robby ventured.

"If you didn't fight, why did you have to leave?" asked the officer.

Sighing, Robby continued, "We broke up and hadn't seen each other for a while—"

"I didn't know he was your boyfriend!" Angelina exclaimed.

"He stayed for about an hour last night," Ellie remarked.

"Long enough to make love," clarified Angelina.

Ellie shot her a censuring glance. "The details aren't important."

"I think it's sweet," Angelina defended.

"Well, the details *might* be important," urged the officer.

"Not *those* details," Ellie assured him.

"Of course not those," Officer Hoffman said. "But what happened after Robby left? What seemed important to you?"

"The two guys outside," Ellie explained, lunging into the saga of her cab ride to the hotel. After describing the men as well as she could, she ended by saying, "I wish I had gotten a better look at them, but it was dark and my mind was on…" Robby. "Other things. The clerk at the hotel might know more about the men, so we could ask him. Last night, I changed my mind about going upstairs to Robby's room, so I turned around and came home, but today it was still bugging me."

"So she came to the hotel again," Robby continued.

Ellie nodded. "I wanted to make sure he knew about the two guys…in case something was wrong."

"And you think your father has something to do with these men?" Officer Hoffman asked.

"Probably," said Robby grimly, "but, naturally, he denied everything when I called him. He's a real piece of work. He actually sounded sincere, even worried."

"If this break-in did have to do with him," the officer speculated out loud, "then why? Is there anything in the office that both he and the other two men would want?"

Ellie shook her head. "Nothing. That's what's so crazy. Nobody would want anything here. All the files contain are hard copies of working papers, mostly printouts of numbers that can be gotten from various available sources, and which I use to make predictions and analyses. Anyone could get these materials. Besides, unless you're a statistician, you wouldn't even know how to read them."

"You do have contracts with companies," Robby said thoughtfully. "Maybe somebody's competition broke in?"

She shrugged. "But why risk getting caught burglarizing? My business arrangements are confidential, but there's nothing high profile right now that might prompt a robbery."

"High profile?" Officer Hoffman questioned.

"Elections, for instance," explained Ellie, "where a third party might want to know my results ahead of time. Those are often announced publicly, anyway. Besides, anything here could be gotten from written requests or downloaded, as I said."

Officer Hoffman blew out a sigh as if to say he was baffled. "Well, I've taken notes, and I'll write up the report. Could each of you possibly come down to the station later and sign it?"

They all nodded. Ellie said, "When?"

"Give me an hour. I'm going to the hotel to question the staff about the gentlemen you mentioned." Officer Hoffman dug into a shirt pocket and handed Ellie a card. "If you think of anything, call me. That's dispatch and a cell."

"Within an hour we should be able to find the floor in here, at least," Angelina remarked. "So if there's something we missed, it may turn up."

"We'll call if we think of anything," Robby added as he showed the officer to the door. When he returned to Ellie's side, he muttered, "I can't imagine what anybody connected to my dad could want in here."

"Maybe your dad isn't involved," she said, her tone softening almost against her will. Shouldn't she be pushing him away once more? she considered, her mind feeling cloudy, her own emotions in turmoil. Still, there was no fighting the sensations of her body. Just looking at him made it come alive; she was abruptly aware of each erogenous zone.

Robby shot her a dubious glance before he began helping the others pick up and straighten the files. "He's involved," he muttered.

"We'll see," Ellie said, as she, too, got on her knees next to him and began to help. He was just a breath away, close enough that the arousing smell of him stirred her blood. It was faint, but she could swear she sensed the faint scent of their lovemaking—a hint of perspiration, some leftover cologne. His muscles rippled pleasantly as he moved, the thighs she'd squeezed between her own stretching the fabric of jeans she suddenly longed to remove. Moments passed in silence, then

Angelina stood and went to the window. "We can touch it now, right?"

"Sure," returned Robby. "When the officer left, he said the forensics people were all done here."

"The window was still open when I came in," Angelina said. "I was so sure I'd shut and locked it when we went for lunch. I think it was those two men you saw. They were probably watching the place and they sound like thugs."

"I hope the cops catch them," offered Antonio. "I can't stand the thought of you two women being here alone after somebody did this."

"Second that emotion," said Robby.

Angelina gasped. "Look!"

Ellie squinted at a small gold object pinched between Angelina's fingers. "What is it?"

"A cuff link."

Ellie rose, moving toward Angelina. "With the initials P.A. engraved on it." Ellie offered a soft whistle when she got a better look. She shut her eyes briefly, trying to remember what the man had worn the previous night. "I can't be sure," she said. "To tell the truth, I didn't pay that much attention to Percy. It wasn't the greatest date," she admitted. Heaving a sigh, she shook her head. "And I always thought my polling skills were so unbeatable. I just don't understand. I have no idea what went wrong. Anyway," she added, "I think Percy was wearing these cuff links, but I can't be certain."

Angelina gasped once more. "I shouldn't have touched it! It might have a fingerprint on it."

"Well, no use crying over spilled milk," Ellie said graciously, "but you need to do me a favor now."

Angelina raised an eyebrow. "What?"

"Call Officer Hoffman and tell him about the cuff link. He's probably almost at the hotel. Tell him we're on our way to Percy's apartment." Going to the desk, she opened a computer file and copied an address for both herself and Angelina, then she jotted Officer Hoffman's number on one of the printout pages and handed it to Angelina. "Percy's place is in Battery Park City, and so is his office."

"You'd better not go," Angelina warned, worriedly pressing her hand to her heart. "You should leave that to the cops."

"I'd go, but I'm not leaving Angelina here alone," announced Antonio. "And I wouldn't want her going to the guy's apartment."

"We'll try his office first," said Ellie.

"They're right, Ellie," Robby said. "Sleuthing is probably better left to the professionals."

"If you want to stay and clean, that's fine by me," Ellie quipped, smiling sweetly at Robby as she grabbed her raincoat and began shrugging into it.

Giving her a playful grin, Robby snagged his jacket from the back of a chair. "Last night, the guy looked pretty harmless. I think I can handle him."

Ellie smiled. "Are you sure you're up to snuff?"

"Earlier some lady seemed to think so."

"Wonder who she was?"

His lips curled teasingly, making her heart swell. Regardless of the future, it felt good to be flirting with Robby Robriquet again. "Gosh, I haven't the faintest idea."

"You two better go," Angelina encouraged. "It's starting to get a bit warm in here."

Ellie laughed as she reached the threshold with Robby next to her, at least until she glanced over her shoulder at Angelina and Antonio. The two were looking at each other, their expressions apprehensive again; they were seemingly engaged in a serious unspoken conversation. When Angelina caught her gaze, the other woman's face rearranged into an unreadable mask. "Be careful," she said.

"We will," Ellie assured her.

But what, if anything, were Antonio and Angelina hiding?

FROM THE BACKSEAT of the cab, Percy kept his gaze on the road and tried not to think about Ellie. In the pockets of his tweed jacket, his hands felt sweaty. One was wrapped around a small knife that had been a gift from his father years ago. He wished he had a more impressive weapon. A knife with a larger blade. Maybe even a gun, not that he really knew how to use one.

Exhaling a worried sigh, he craned his head and checked behind him, damning himself for the mess he'd made of his life. "And the look on Helen Wharton's face!" he whispered, cringing.

He visualized his desk at the accounting firm, and Helen bustling around it. Earlier, she'd shot him a look so full of heartfelt concern. She was so pretty. Not glamorous like Ellie, of course, but...more caring. Ellie had turned his head, but after the rush of emotions surrounding their date had worn off, his mind had surprisingly returned to Helen. She was plump, and if Percy was honest, he liked that. He imagined running his palms over her full hips, then stopped the fantasy. That was never going to happen. Face it, he was in a cab heading for danger, his sweating hand wrapped around a damn penknife.

The weapon was all he had. That, and a determination to end this farce. He'd done what he'd been told to do, and broken into Ellie's apartment, but he was doing no more favors for Joey, Jimmy and their boss, Big Frank. Big Frank would get the money Percy owed when Percy could deliver. Meantime, he wanted to make sure Ellie wasn't in danger.

Wincing, he saw Helen Wharton's plain concerned face wavering in his consciousness. No, she wasn't beautiful, but she had soft, curly dark hair that any man would want to touch. "When it rains, it pours," Percy muttered.

In his whole life, he'd scarcely had one woman to worry about, and now he had two. Even worse, the mob was essentially blackmailing him, forcing him into illegal activities because he owed them money he couldn't pay. When had his life gotten so exciting? Right about now, he just wanted his old life back, with no gambling troubles and no women.

What if he did go with Helen Wharton? Would Ellie get over it? His hand tightened around the knife. Only time would tell.

11

"PULL OVER," Ellie instructed the driver from the backseat of a cab. To Robby, she continued, "Look, Percy's going inside." The man ducked inside a gray door with a small window near the top, the kind of door she'd expect to see at an old speakeasy. Ellie and Robby had arrived at Percy's accounting office just in time to see him grab a cab, so they'd followed him to this street; it could have belonged to either Soho or Little Italy, but it was hard to tell which.

Robby handed the driver some bills.

As he accepted the fare, the man stared between Ellie and Robby. "I don't think you should go in."

Ellie frowned. "Why not?"

"It's a social club."

"Social club?" Ellie echoed.

"The mob," Robby muttered. "Thanks for telling us," he added as he and Ellie got out.

"No problem," the cabbie called as the door slammed shut.

"You stay here," Robby said as soon as they were both on the sidewalk.

"This can't be a mob hangout. Percy is hardly the mob type," Ellie said nervously, taking in the deserted street; most of the buildings were warehouses.

"Stay here anyway. If I'm not back in ten minutes, call Officer Hoffman."

"I'll call him anyway, since he won't know where to find us now."

After quickly kissing her, Robby was gone, his long legs eating up the pavement as she punched in a number for the officer. The policeman picked up immediately.

"Hello?"

"It's Ellie Lee. You were at my apartment earlier?"

"Yes. What can I do for you? You'll be pleased to know I just got some interesting information from the clerk at the hotel. He remembers you well. Also, the men whose description you gave. He said they paid him for Robby's full name, home address and room number."

Her eyes darted to the door Robby had just entered. "Oh, my God," she whispered, her heart hammering.

"I need to show the clerk some mug shots," the officer continued, "but he said he saw a stain on the side of the neck of one of the men."

"A stain?"

"A birthmark."

"I didn't notice, but it was dark." Ellie's eyes were still glued to the door of the social club. "But right now, I just want you to know that—"

Officer Hoffman cut her off. "Given the description of the birthmark, I think it's a guy named Joey D. He hangs around with his brother, Jimmy C. The C and D refer to their middle names. Joey's the larger of the two, but since they're brothers, they otherwise look alike. They work for a mobster named Big Frank."

Ellie felt weak. As Officer Hoffman had spoken, she'd spotted a woman at the end of the block. Plain-looking and a little chubby with curly dark hair, the woman was wearing a lightweight coat and clutching a pocketbook. For a second, Ellie thought the lady had been watching her, but she glanced down the street, as if she was looking for a cab.

"Are you okay?" It was Officer Hoffman.

"No," Ellie said urgently. She rattled off the door number nearest her and the cross streets. Quickly, she explained what had happened, beginning with Angelina's finding the cuff link. "Robby just went inside," she finished.

"Stay put. Do not go in there. I'm on my way."

"Hurry," Ellie urged before punching a button to end the call and pocketing her phone. Slowly, she approached the door. The window was toward the top, but if she stood on her tiptoes, maybe she could peer inside.

The pulse wild in her throat, she raised herself up, now glad she'd worn high heels even though they were pinching her feet. There were men inside, dressed in black, wearing baseball caps. They were playing cards and didn't notice her. Given their appearance, she hoped they didn't. Sure enough, now she could see that the larger one had a birthmark on the side of his neck.

"Jimmy and Joey," she whispered, wishing she had a weapon. Beyond them, a door was cracked open and she could see Percy's and Robby's backs. They were talking to a huge man with dark hair and full lips who was wearing a tan suit.

All at once, the larger of the two men in baseball caps, Joey, twisted in his chair as if he'd heard something of interest from the next room. Fanning his cards on the table, he rose, a hand moving to his hip. "Not a good sign," Ellie murmured.

Her chest was burning now. It was as if the air she was breathing had turned to fire. Without thinking, she pushed through the door, danger be damned. Officer Hoffman would be here any second, and she had to help Robby.

Joey spun around.

"What are you doing here, lady?" The smaller man rose to his feet.

Just as she was about to respond, she spied through the

crack in the interior door and saw Percy whip out a knife, threatening the seated man. "Look here, Big Frank, I'm not paying you another damn dime," Percy declared. "Not now, not ever. You'll get what I owe you when I have it."

As if compelled to move by an unseen hand, Ellie crept forward. "Percy?"

He peered through the crack, which widened as Robby further opened the door. "Ellie! Get outside!"

Too late. Robby met her gaze, looking furious that she'd followed him. The door behind her swung open and every-body turned toward the newcomer. But Ellie's relief was short-lived. It wasn't Officer Hoffman, but the dark-haired woman she'd seen on the street. With a quick glance, Ellie summed her up as a tourist. She must have seen Ellie come inside, so she'd figured the place wasn't dangerous. Probably she couldn't find a cab on this block and was looking for a phone.

"Helen?" Percy pushed his wire-frame glasses farther up on the bridge of his nose with his knife-free hand. "Oh, no. What are you doing here? Please go outside."

The woman came to Ellie's side. "I'm not leaving until I make sure you're okay," she said tremulously. Looking down, she opened the clasp to her pocketbook and withdrew a handful of papers. "I've been finding these racing forms for some time. In your pockets, in your desk drawers and even in folders for meetings. I know I'm just an assistant, and it's not my business, but you could never be a gambler at heart, Percy. I know you've had some personal problems, but you need help and whether you like me or not, Percy Anders, I am here to help you."

Ellie could only stare at the woman. She looked utterly ter-rified, but just as determined to protect Percy. "You're Percy's assistant?"

"Yes, indeed. I do work for the firm."

"Please, Helen," Percy pleaded, glancing between Helen, Ellie and the man on whom he was holding the knife, "Wait outside."

"No," Helen said adamantly. "My good conscience will not allow that."

Fortunately, none of the mobsters seemed genuinely threatened by Percy's weapon or anyone else in the room—except Robby. Jimmy and Joey were remaining cognizant of his every move, which was probably wise. Often, when they were kids, Ellie had seen Robby brawl with her brothers and he usually won.

Percy's eyes were focused on Ellie. "I'm sorry, Ellie," he continued. "I don't have anything formal going on with Helen, I can assure you of that. I don't two-time."

"I know you like her more," Helen put in, now looking as if she was fighting tears. "But I want to help you. You're such a nice man. When I first came on the job, I misfiled some papers pertaining to the Lee Polls account. You remember how we hired them, to find out how to better serve our customers?"

"Lee Polls?" Percy frowned. "No...I didn't know we used them."

"Well, we did. And I got yelled at by one of the top executives, but you told me not to worry a bit. You've always been so sweet and kind to me..."

"And I do like you," Percy gushed. "I like you more than Ellie, so don't worry about that."

Helen gasped. "You do?"

Ellie stared at him. "You do?"

Just then, the door opened again, and everyone turned to stare once more. Angelina and Antonio burst inside breathlessly, and Angelina looked as though she'd been crying, too.

"I have something I have to tell you, Ellie," she began in a rush. "I'm so sorry. I know you're going to fire me, and I don't blame you! You're well within your rights!"

"What is going on here?" Robby muttered.

"I'd like to know, too," said Big Frank. "My social club is turning into a three-ring circus."

"What's going on is that I can't give you the money now, Big Frank." Percy looked at Ellie. "I've been gambling, and I can't pay what I owe, so these two guys—" Percy jerked his head in the direction of Jimmy and Joey "—told me they might harm you if I didn't break into your office and look for information about how you make such good judgment calls. They wanted your tricks of the trade, to predict wins and losses in gambling games."

"It wasn't me who was most interested in Ms. Lee," Big Frank countered, now looking down at his hands and studying them. "I owed a guy a favor, that's all."

"What guy?" Percy demanded.

"For me to know," Big Frank crooned.

"Max Sweeney," Robby guessed.

Big Frank's head shot up, and he gave Robby a hard look. Now Big Frank looked dangerous, his eyes dark and beady, his large body clearly made up of muscle not fat. "What do you know about Max Sweeney?"

"Unfortunately, we share a town in Mississippi," Robby drawled, sounding lethal.

"What's a Southern fellow like you doing all the way up here?" asked Big Frank.

"Following a trail," returned Robby.

"Who's Max Sweeney?" Percy asked, clearly dumbfounded.

"A bookie in Ellie's hometown," Robby informed him. "One who somehow knows this jerk." He gestured to Big Frank, and in a quick, seamless motion, Robby lunged, grabbing the knife from Percy's hand. In a second, he was behind Big Frank, holding the knife to the man's carotid artery. His eyes fixed on Joey and Jimmy. "Don't even think about moving," Robby warned.

The other two men waited cautiously.

Big Frank raised both his hands, palms out, as if he didn't have a care in the world. "If the truth be told, Max Sweeney isn't even one of my favorite people," he assured them. "So do me a favor and put down the knife, would you? I owe him a favor, a very small favor," Big Frank qualified. "And so he asked me to figure out how this young lady made such good predictions. Since it turned out she was dating a man who owes *me* a healthy sum, I figured he might be useful in my quest."

"You ever hurt her," Robby warned. "And you're a dead man."

"No need to threaten me," Big Frank assured him. "Jeesh."

"You can dish danger out, but you sure can't take it," muttered Ellie. "And by the way, the police just left my office. They'll be here any second."

"You never should have tried to use Percy like that," Helen spit out venomously, her dark curls flying as she tossed her head defiantly. "He's a good man and he just needs help."

Big Frank shrugged. He was staring at Ellie. "How do you make such good judgment calls, anyway?"

Something was niggling at Ellie. Had Percy's firm really hired Lee Polls in the past? She started to ask for clarification, but this was hardly the time. Instead, she glared at Frank. "How do I do it?" she echoed. "Try college, hard work and experience, buster."

Big Frank looked shocked. "No kidding?"

"No kidding," Ellie returned.

"College?" Big Frank repeated, shaking his head as if he couldn't quite believe formal education was capable of rendering any positive results in the real world. Suddenly conscious once more of the knife at his throat, he quit moving his head. "No tricks, you swear?"

"None," Ellie said, gaping at the man. "On my honor. You collect data and analyze it. That's all."

"Well, I'll be damned." Big Frank seemed impressed despite the knife Robby still held at his neck. "And what kind of degree did you get?"

"You can research that for yourself, Big Frank," muttered Ellie. Hearing something behind her, Ellie turned just in time to see Officer Hoffman. "Officer," she said.

"Everybody get back," he said calmly, his hand on his belt, hovering near his weapon. "Jimmy and Joey, down on the floor. Ladies, you go outside."

Only Helen and Angelina moved, with Antonio following, as Robby lowered the knife.

"No hard feelings," Big Frank said casually to no one in particular.

Robby handed the knife to Percy, who closed and pocketed it, then Robby began explaining the situation to the officer, who listened as he called for backup. "You three are going to the precinct," Officer Hoffman said.

"For what?" Big Frank laughed. "It was this fellow—" he pointed to Percy "—who broke into the young lady's office."

"Incitement to robbery," Officer Hoffman said. "Blackmail, if that's how you coerced Percy."

"I did break in," Percy admitted, "and I intend to make just restitution."

"Oh, don't worry about it," muttered Ellie, deciding it would be sheer lunacy to press charges. Not to mention bad business, since the man was supposed to be her dream lover, as far as the public was concerned. Percy was a loser, but her gut told her he was trying to straighten out his screwed-up life. Besides, he'd come here to protect her. Legal action against him wouldn't help matters nearly as much as the loving care of his assistant, Helen.

"No dice," said Officer Hoffman. "But I trust you to go outside and not make a run for it. In my opinion, you'll merely wind up doing community service."

Percy appeared relieved. "I'll be right outside with Helen," he promised, "ready to make my confession at any time."

Ellie noticed Robby. His gaze was roving over her, as if to make sure she was okay. "I need a breath of fresh air," she announced.

"Go on outside," Robby returned. "I'll help Officer Hoffman watch these goons until backup arrives."

Surely, Officer Hoffman would want to bring any possible charges against the three remaining men in whatever way he could, if only to build a rap sheet, Ellie figured. It might come in handy when these three got into more serious trouble, which they would, given their recent shenanigans with Percy. They'd used him and made death threats. Probably the officer was right about giving Percy community service, too. Years of living around a man as devious as her father had likely made her too much of a soft touch, Ellie decided.

"What a world," she whispered as she stepped into the sunlight. Just as she drew a calming breath, Angelina came up to her, swiping tears from her eyes.

"You're never going to forgive me," she began.

Ellie placed a hand on the sleeve of the other woman's coat. "What are you so upset about? Don't worry about having left the window open. It's all okay now."

"It's more than that." Angelina glanced at Antonio, who had come to stand beside her. "I did something awful. I didn't think it would matter, not like this."

So Ellie's gut had been right. Angelina and Antonio were hiding something. She frowned. "What did you do?"

"Rigged the results of the poll," Angelina confessed in a rush. "Do you remember how, when you conducted the poll to find Mr. Right, you gave each man a numerical code that would identify him?"

Ellie nodded slowly.

"Well, I'm the one who really chose the winner, by switching the names and numbers."

"Percy wasn't the person I chose from the random data?" Striving for objectivity, she had never had names attached to the men, only numbers.

Angelina's voice trembled and her shoulders shook as if she were withholding sobs. "The papers revealing the correct person are hidden in my lowest desk drawer on the left-hand side. And I deleted the man's name and number from the sequence in the computers. I'm so sorry!"

Ellie couldn't believe it. "Angelina…why?"

Antonio put a protective arm around Angelina as she began weeping. "She thought we could use the money. She wanted us to have the perfect wedding," he explained.

"And I thought the change would make you happy! I didn't think you had any other boyfriend! I thought I was matchmaking! I thought Percy was your real boyfriend from the past! So I put in his data, switching his number with that of another man, so it would look as if he was the right person. And… and…" Angelina couldn't bring herself to continue.

"She agreed to take five thousand dollars for doing it," Antonio explained, ever ready to defend her.

"I just wanted the best wedding ever," Angelina howled.

"I know that, sweetie," Antonio crooned. "You love me and I love you, and everything is going to be just fine. Don't worry."

"I thought it was the right thing to do!"

Ellie's mind could barely catch up. "Somebody was going to pay you five thousand dollars to put Percy's name forward?" She could only shake her head. "At least the problem wasn't my statistical skills. I never make mistakes."

"Percy wasn't the right man?" Helen was edging closer with Percy on her heels.

"I wasn't?" asked Percy.

Angelina shook her head. "I don't know who was. I didn't look at his name."

Ellie barely heard Angelina, since she was seeing red. Only her father could be this sneaky. But why on earth would he set her up on a date with Percy Anders? "You said Lee Polls did some work for your accounting firm?"

Helen nodded. "Yes."

"I never knew that," said Percy. Speaking only to Helen, he continued, "I remember that day you got into trouble at work, but I didn't know what kind of papers you were filing." Before she could answer, he added, "And don't worry. I'll make sure no other bosses waylay you in the future." He smiled. "You're mine and mine alone."

"You mean it?" Helen gushed.

"I sure do. Why, Helen, I knew you liked me, but I've made such a disaster of my life lately that I didn't feel I deserved you. I just hope Ellie…"

"Don't worry about me," Ellie managed. "I promise to make no claim on you."

Percy looked relieved. "Thank you, Ellie."

"No problem." Her gaze landed on Angelina again. "You said somebody paid you to skew the results of the poll and set me up with Percy. Who?"

"He said he was your dad."

That didn't surprise Ellie in the least, but it was the exact wrong moment for more policemen to arrive and race inside. A second later, Robby came out and slung his arm around Ellie. Yes…it was the wrong time to feel his hot hands and remember them roving all over her body. Until last night, she thought she'd never again feel his warm tongue working its velvet magic on her choicest parts, nor the well-being she experienced when he wrapped his arms around her and held her tight.

Even now, the memory was enough to send lightning flashes of desire through her body. She was recalling his mouth on her breasts, his hands tracing her curves, and most of all, how hard and good he'd felt buried deep inside her. But now, all those sweet things just added up to another betrayal. "It was one thing for you to come here with that proposal you and Daddy Eddie cooked up," she started.

"Whoa," Robby said in surprise. "What, Ellie?"

"You know damn well what I'm talking about. Offering me Daddy Eddie's proposal was one thing, but then you had sex with me, no doubt to soften me on the deal which, by the way, I know Lee Polls really needs."

"We'll survive without it," Robby said dryly, his demeanor changing, his jaw becoming harder, his eyes piercing.

"You, personally, will have to survive without me, too. Maybe I could have dealt with most things you've done, Robby, but being a party to Daddy's scheme to tamper with the results of my poll, just so that I'd wind up with Percy when I wasn't supposed to…I just can't get past that."

Robby was looking at her as if he'd never seen her before. "And there we have it," he announced. "The level of your trust."

"Why would I trust you, much less Daddy Eddie?"

"Oh, no," Angelina interjected, crying. "Don't break up on my account! It was your dad who told me to switch the results, Ellie, not him. And your dad hasn't actually sent me the money. I won't take it, of course. I quit, too. You could never forgive me and I fully understand." Whatever else she was going to say was lost as she was now sobbing. Antonio held her in his arms.

Helen and Percy had drifted away. They were halfway down the block, locked in an embrace. Everybody was a happy couple, except Ellie and Robby. Even Susannah, Ellie's best friend, had reconciled with her husband. Ellie's hand moved to her neck to touch the charm she wore. As she did so, she visualized the words engraved there: Remember the Time.

Memories were all she was going to have left. After Robby was gone, she'd never forget the heat in his kisses, nor the confident power of his lovemaking. She glanced at Angelina and Antonio, then Percy and Helen, and then she thought of Susannah and J.D. once more. Some couples had all the luck.

Robby was glaring at her. "You think I skewed the results of your poll?"

"Daddy Eddie obviously did the dirty work, but this one shows the fine touch of your business acumen, something I've come to respect over the years, at least in other circumstances. What?" she suddenly demanded. "Were you hoping to discredit my skills by making me look like a fool in front of Derrick Mills and the media?"

Robby's blue eyes were flashing. "You know," he muttered. "You have a far more devious mind than me."

"I doubt that."

"You're exactly like your father."

It was the same accusation she'd aimed at Robby months before, not that she was going to remind him that his own dad was a murderer. But then, maybe Charlie had changed. As it turned out, he hadn't been involved in what had just transpired. No, she thought, feeling a jolt of temper, the culprits had been her father and lover.

"I could have gotten worse genes than Daddy Eddie's," she defended. "He's manipulative, but at least he's a good businessman." Unlike Charlie, she thought, letting the silence speak.

Robby seemed in the throes of warring emotions he could barely contain. A hand half lifted, as if he was going to stroke her cheek, but he didn't. "I can't take this, Ellie."

"Take what?" As usual, she was in the wrong! He'd taken her job, then had the audacity to show up on the doorstep with a business deal, then he'd hustled her into bed when she'd refused the merger. Now it was likely he'd been a party to botching her poll, perhaps in an attempt to make her look bad. "*You* can't take this?"

"No," he said simply.

"Then leave," she suggested.

"I will."

And with that, he turned on his heel and strode down the sidewalk toward Percy and Helen. Later, Ellie imagined, she'd feel more heartbreak, but she was used to that. Dammit, as far as Robby Robriquet was concerned, she'd been feeling heartbreak for a lifetime.

Suddenly, she realized he'd left his duffel bag at her apartment. He definitely wouldn't be spending the night. Tears welled, making her eyelids feel heavy and swollen. He hadn't even kissed her goodbye, nor offered a backward glance. As he reached the corner and thrust out his arm to hail a cab, she almost couldn't believe their relationship was over.

A cab appeared immediately, which was amazing, given the desolate block. He got in, shut the door and the car sped away. She doubted he'd go to her place for the bag. The door was locked and there was no one home to give it to him.

Was she never going to see him again? Could that really be for the best? This ending seemed so undramatic. They hadn't even had a knock-down, drag-out fight. There were no real tears or fireworks—and, as crazy as it sounded, she felt her and Robby's affair deserved something more passionate.

She heard the door open behind her and turned. Policemen were coming outside with the three handcuffed men. Officer Hoffman stopped beside her. "I'm going to need you all to come to the precinct and give a statement."

She looked at him, barely able to collect her thoughts. "Robby just left."

Officer Hoffman's chin came up sharply. "Robby Robriquet? Who was with you a second ago?"

Alarm shot through her. What was wrong? "Yes, why?"

Officer Hoffman exhaled as if to say it was going to be a very long day. Flipping through his book, he glanced at her once more and said, "From Banner, Mississippi?"

"That's where we're from."

"Hmm. Do you know Charlie Robriquet?"

"Sure do." Her heart sank. She was angry at Robby, yes, but she ached for him now, because his father must have been involved with this, after all. Why else would the officer have learned his name? Max Sweeney had been his bookie in the past, so maybe they had reconnected. "He's Robby's dad."

Officer Hoffman wolf whistled. "On my way here from the hotel, I got a call from a fellow named Sheriff Kemp."

"Sheriff Kemp?" He had called the New York police? "I know him. Why did he call?"

"Apparently, Robby called his father, Charlie, and sparked a chain reaction. As it turns out, Max Sweeney, the guy Big Frank knows, has a son."

"Johnny. I never knew him well. He was older than me and Robby." A real jerk, too. Max had bought everything under the sun for him, spoiling him rotten. The only saving grace was that Max wound up raising exactly the adult he deserved. Johnny still raced around town in fancy sports cars, drinking and womanizing. He was not a nice guy.

"Well…years ago, Robby's father got himself into much the same situation as Percy Anders just did with Big Frank," Officer Hoffman said. "Except it was Max Sweeney who had him over a barrel."

That was old news. "How do Big Frank and Max know each other?" she asked.

"According to information I just got, they met in Atlantic City. Both of them take frequent trips there."

"As they would. It feels like a coincidence, but I guess it's not. My dad was hired by Percy's accounting firm, he tried to hook me up with Percy as a result, and Percy turned out to be a gambler like Charlie."

"Gambling is a sickness," Officer Hoffman said. "So it's hardly special. Lots of people do have it."

"Nobody I want to know," Ellie remarked. "What were you saying about Charlie and Max?"

"Robby's call set off a series of events. His father was really upset. Turns out, he'd owed Max a lot of money in the past."

"He always did."

"So one night, Max's kid, the one you mentioned, Johnny, had an accident, so Max tried to frame Charlie for it. When that didn't work well enough, he threatened Charlie and got him to confess to a killing."

"Of Shirley Fey?" Ellie's lips parted in shock. "Charlie didn't run her over in the road?"

"It was Johnny Sweeney."

Her mind was racing, thinking over the various conflicting stories Charlie had offered at the time. People had thought he was confused or drunk. If he hadn't been the perpetrator of the crime, though, it was no wonder there were so many discrepancies in the case. "He wouldn't confess to a crime like that just to erase gambling debts," she said.

Officer Hoffman shook his head. "Nope. Max Sweeney threatened the life of Charlie's son, Robby, if Charlie didn't take the rap."

Ellie reached out and grabbed the officer's arm to steady herself. "Charlie was in jail for eight years! Are you saying he confessed to a crime to save Robby's life?"

"Unless he's lying now. And since he's already done the time, he has no reason not to tell the truth. He swears Max visited him in jail frequently, vowing to kill Robby if Charlie ever said a word."

Ellie thought of Charlie. Years of alcohol use had come in the wake of his wife's death, leaving him weak, so unlike his son. Sadly, the story seemed plausible. Ellie wouldn't put anything past Max Sweeney. He was the scum of the earth. She felt sick. If it was true, Robby would be shaken to the core. And she felt terrible for his dad. He might not be Banner's most upstanding citizen, but he'd done time without the crime. "Why did he come forward now?"

"The call he got from his Robby. Charlie felt he'd done everything right, to the letter, just as Max Sweeney requested. He'd done the time for Johnny for years. But then, as soon as he got out of jail, he found out goons were following Robby, anyway. Not only that, but it seemed you might be in danger, as well. I guess he realized that when you're dealing with thugs, the attacks never end. There's no honor among thieves. That's a myth. You give them an inch and they always take a mile.

"So he went to Sheriff Kemp and spilled his guts, hoping to protect both of you," Officer Hoffman continued. "Turns out, the sheriff never thought Charlie committed the crime, and he's waited all these years for new information to surface."

"Everybody around town had doubts about it, but with the

forensic evidence left by Max Sweeney at the scene of Shirley Fey's death, the jury had no choice but to convict Charlie," Ellie said.

"In truth, we suspect Shirley went on a date with Johnny Sweeney," Officer Hoffman explained. "Maybe they argued and that's why she got out of the car and started to walk home and he ran over her. It must have been an accident. Manslaughter," he clarified. "Not murder one. In my line of work, you see this kind of scenario a lot."

Glancing around, Ellie noted the other two couples had left, probably deciding not to wait since she'd been in deep conversation with the officer. No doubt, they'd find their own way to the precinct to make their statements.

"Unbelievable," she finally whispered. Lifting her gaze, she searched the street, half expecting Robby to reappear, but of course he didn't.

And then she burst into tears.

12

ANGELINA HAD JUST walked out the door. Seeing Ellie, she lifted a hand, palm out. "I don't expect you to ever speak to me again. My resignation is on the desk."

Ellie's mind was still reeling with the news about Charlie as she took in her assistant's rumpled hair, probably mussed from Antonio's fingers. Angelina's eyes were red-rimmed, and she looked miserable. "Don't be silly," Ellie said. Leaning in, she gave the other woman a quick hug. "You're not resigning. I need you more than ever."

"You do?"

Angelina looked so overwhelmed by guilt that Ellie's heart tugged with sympathy. "Absolutely. Take the rest of the day off and come back tomorrow when you feel better. There's nothing going on here that can't wait. It's been a long day. Where's Antonio?"

"Waiting in the car." Angelina nodded toward the curb.

Ellie waved at him. "I'll see you tomorrow."

"Your dad was trying to make you happy, I think," Angelina ventured.

"You only believe that because you've never met Daddy Eddie," Ellie said dryly. "He can be very persuasive."

"He was playing matchmaker. That's how it seemed."

"Don't use your mental energy worrying about Daddy Eddie's motivations. It's a waste of time. I'll take care of him." In fact, it was the first thing Ellie was going to do when she got inside. "Did Robby come back?"

Angelina shook her head. "No."

Ellie wished her heart hadn't lurched. Dammit, only now did she realize she'd half hoped he'd be waiting for her on the stoop. "Now, go on," she said. "You and Antonio have a great night."

"Thank you," Angelina said guiltily.

Ellie headed inside and for the phone. If she got her way, Daddy Eddie would be giving Angelina and Antonio the five thousand dollars he'd promised as a wedding gift. Lifting the receiver on the landline, she punched in the number for Daddy Eddie's direct line at Lee Polls.

As she waited for him to answer, her eyes swept the room. Angelina had cleaned quite a bit, including wiping away the residue left by the fingerprinting team, but there would still be a lot of work to do tomorrow. Her heart wrenched when her eyes landed on Robby's duffel on the floor. Instinctively, her fingers closed over the charm on her necklace. "Remember the time," she whispered.

So many memories. She and Susannah, along with Robby and J. D. Johnson, had experienced such wonderful times, Christmases and Easters, sledding and fishing. And there was all the great sex she'd shared with Robby. Now…she was left with nothing more than an old duffel. Tears welled in her eyes, but she held them back. "Dammit, Daddy Eddie, where are you?"

Maybe he'd seen her number on caller I.D. and was too afraid to pick up. The story Officer Hoffman told about Robby's dad had been nothing short of astonishing, Ellie thought now. She hadn't heard much about Sheriff Kemp lately, either, and just hearing a name from her old town had made her homesick.

She also missed Banner Manor, the historic family home

Susannah shared with J.D. Oh, Ellie wanted her old friends back, her old life, her old haunts. Swallowing around a lump in her throat, she wondered where Robby had gone.

Because the man had betrayed her one too many times, she wasn't going to chase after him, of course. Being in cahoots with Daddy Eddie's scheme to skew her poll was the icing on the cake.

Abruptly, the phone clicked on. "Hello?"

"Daddy?"

There was a long pause. "Ellie?"

"Yeah, it's me."

Another long pause ensued. Suddenly, Daddy Eddie spoke in a rush, as he often did. "I know how much you hate me, so it must be one heck of an emergency."

"I don't hate you," she muttered, her eyes on Robby's duffel once more. She felt an urge to open it and smell some of his shirts. "Well…maybe I hate you a little," Ellie amended. "My assistant says you wanted to pay her five thousand dollars to tamper with my poll results."

"All is fair in love and war," Daddy Eddie chided, not even bothering to deny it.

Too late. She knew she shouldn't have told her father she didn't hate him. Now he thought he had her over a barrel. "You're the one who started all this," she accused. "You gave my promotion to Robby."

"It was mine to give as I saw fit."

True enough. And in the past twenty-four hours, Ellie hadn't cared, at least not when she'd been in Robby's arms again. Yet she knew this was about more than just the job. Robby had known about the promotion, yet he'd made love to her, anyway. She simply couldn't have the kind of relationship where they withheld information from each other. She'd observed that tendency to keep secrets in Robby before, but she'd written it off as a response to the distrust he'd felt during his chaotic childhood.

Daddy Eddie's voice broke her reverie. "Well, I'm glad you see the wisdom in my decision."

"I didn't say that! And for all the trouble you caused Future Trends," she added, "I expect you to pay Angelina for her services, since she corrupted my data, just as you asked. You also caused her mental duress, but if you give her the money, so she can use it for her wedding, I won't sue. Furthermore, I had to endure a date with Percy Anders and now, I don't know what I'm going to tell the media."

"Why, that's a long list of problems," Daddy Eddie said, chortling happily. "It's a good thing your old man is such a whiz at business. So, since you learned from him, and got all his business-related genes, I'm confident you'll meet those challenges with true ingenuity."

"Hmm. Ever the egotist," she proclaimed. "Your shenanigans led to the robbery of my office, Daddy Eddie, not to mention a run-in with the mob. And if you keep on vexing me, I'm going to stoop to telling Mama on you."

"Fine. I'm sure you'll do whatever you see fit. I wouldn't be involved at all, but some officer named Hoffman called Sheriff Kemp, then he called me to tell me all about this mess you were in."

"I'm in a mess!" she exclaimed. He'd created it!

"I was at Delia's Diner at the time," her father plunged on. "The sheriff's dating Delia nowadays, but I bet you didn't know that, since you're so far away from home in the big city. We've been having a wonderful time here, by the by. Why, Delia had a party for Sheriff Kemp's birthday, and I heard Susannah's sister might be pregnant again."

A strange poignancy swept over Ellie. It had been a while since she'd heard one of Daddy Eddie's trademark monologues. Talking until people gave into his demands had always been one of his better strategies. "When you talk like this," she said, "I know it's only because you're angling for something."

"Now, that's silly, Ellie. And I'm sorry for rambling, but I'm getting old and I don't even have any heirs. And I should have known my busy daughter had no interest in community gossip. Here…wait a second while I take a bite of Delia's coconut pie, which I brought back to the office to eat for desert. Hmm-hmm. Why, this pie has always been one of my favorites. But then, everything Delia makes is good. Although not as good as your mama makes."

Daddy Eddie lowered his voice. "Maybe I shouldn't say so, but your mama misses you. I don't—oh, I admit it. I've got plenty else on my mind."

"Yeah, like ruining my life!" she interjected.

"Maybe, but you know how your mother is! Why, just the other day, Patricia turned to me and she said, 'Daddy Eddie, I was just thinking about our baby girl—'"

"If you're trying to make me homesick," Ellie interjected, "it's not working!"

"Isn't it?" Daddy Eddie crooned.

"No!"

"Then why are you so upset?" he asked, his voice all innocent.

He had a point. The fact was, she felt heart-wrenching homesickness all the time. "Daddy," she suddenly said, "why did you give that job to Robby?"

"All in good time, my dear."

"Don't start pulling your cryptic wise-man routine."

"You should trust your elders."

"Meaning?"

"Father knows best."

Before she could say anything more, he continued. "And

I think a break from teeny-tiny old Banner, Mississippi, has done wonders for you. If you do start feeling lonely, it's probably because you're starting to remember the poor, pitiful things you left behind. I'm not talking about your family and friends or the public eateries and our quaint library and the beauty of our town's Christmas decorations. Oh, maybe that means nothing to you now. Why, you're having big-city adventures complete with home invasions and mobsters with names such as Big Frank!"

"Daddy, that's your fault!"

"Well, I'm just sorry Percy Anders didn't work out to be your dream man."

"Why did you pick him of all people?"

"I didn't. If the truth be told, his name was on a long list of employee names from an accounting firm where I was doing business."

Her father was completely insane. "He could have been a stalker or a crazy person!"

"All the employees at the accountancy firm are thoroughly vetted. I did check that. So I knew you were safe."

"He wasn't safe! He had a gambling problem!"

"Men aren't what they used to be," Daddy Eddie commiserated. "If you want my opinion—"

"I don't!"

"As I was saying before you interrupted," Daddy Eddie pushed on, "feminism has damn near ruined all the good guys. They're so sensitive now. Hardly anybody seems to hunt and fish and target shoot."

"Hunt and fish and target shoot!" she exclaimed. "You always act like you're the one who's marrying them!"

"You're getting married?" he queried, his voice curious.

He was impossible. "No!"

"Good, because I'd never want to deal with a son-in-law

who couldn't handle at least a twelve gauge, if only so he could protect you."

"This is hardly the Stone Age! Protect me from what?"

"Yourself."

"I can take care of myself. And what was your point in tampering with my data, Daddy? Did you want me to have a lousy date? Or look incompetent as a statistician? Or to embarrass me publicly?"

"You certainly think highly of me." Now he sounded injured.

Sighing in frustration, she plopped into the desk chair. "How does Mama ever deal with you?"

"I'm nicer to your mother," confessed Daddy Eddie.

"Okay, try being nice to me!" Still wearing her raincoat, she hugged it to herself. Too bad the heat hadn't come back on. "I don't appreciate your sabotaging my business," she said firmly.

"Boys will be boys. And who knows? It could have worked out. Don't you want to get married someday? Have a family? A nice house? Oh…I forgot. You already had a cute house, but your mother is taking care of it, since her capricious daughter abandoned her own home. She got on a plane and left town without so much as a goodbye! Well, I guess such a lifestyle wouldn't include a man."

"Not Percy Anders, anyway."

"Maybe there are other fish in the sea."

As dejected as she felt, Daddy Eddie was almost making her smile. Almost. But Robby's abandoned duffel was still in her living room and the man wasn't coming back. "Next time, don't send me the shrimp."

Daddy Eddie chortled. "No bottom-feeders?"

"Percy was more of a weasel."

"Those don't do well in the sea, I hear."

"You're the fisherman."

"I am, indeed. In fact, I just got a new rod, so your ex-colleague and I went fishing yesterday. Remember Robby Robriquet? Such a nice fellow! It's warmer here than where you are, I suspect, so we got a fine catch. Took trout home to Mama and she fried them for our supper."

Kicking off her shoes, Ellie flexed her feet. If she'd known she was going to walk so much, she wouldn't have worn high heels. Pulling out a lower desk drawer, she used the edge as a footstool and propped her feet on it. "That's impossible," Ellie said dryly, glad to catch her father in another of his lies.

Daddy Eddie sounded genuinely surprised. "Why?"

"Because Robby was here. He brought your business proposal for merging Lee Polls and Future Trends."

There was a long silence. Then Daddy Eddie exploded. "Impossible! We batted around an idea, but I never developed it. He can't merge my company with another without my say so!"

Ellie was enjoying this. "Hmm, you did make him president, so I suppose he feels he can do whatever he wishes."

"It's my company still."

"You should have thought of that before you retired."

"I didn't retire! There's too much work around here for Robby to do it on his own!"

Ellie had suspected as much. "Sorry to hear that," she crooned sweetly. "But Robby sure left the impression the deal he offered was your handiwork."

"Robby's in the Caribbean, Ellie."

This time her father actually sounded serious. "Really?"

"He's been gone a week."

So Robby really had worked on the deal behind her dad's back and brought it here. Deep down, she suspected it had been a ploy to get her to go home. She knew her family missed her. She still wasn't sure she should believe her father. "Why would Robby go to the Caribbean?"

"Vacation. It's been tough here, Ellie. You're giving your old man a real run for his money. You took half our clients."

It was an exaggeration, but she let it pass because her father suddenly sounded old and tired. Just hearing his shift in tone broke her heart. "It's a good deal," she found herself saying. "I'm still considering it."

"Can I talk to Robby?"

"He's gone."

"Gone?"

She nodded, staring at Angelina's resignation letter on the desk. Once more, her heart squeezed, since the letter was chock-full of compliments about how much Angelina had enjoyed helping Ellie build Future Trends. It didn't help that one of her bridal magazines was right beneath the letter, either.

Unbidden, Ellie recalled the rush of sensation she always felt when her body merged with Robby's. Every inch of the man was honed, as hard as rock and as solid as steel. "We got into a fight," she confided. "I thought you'd put him up to coming here, so naturally, I also assumed he'd had a hand in skewing my poll results."

"No!" Daddy Eddie exploded. "He didn't! And Robby didn't tell me anything about the deal."

That meant he, too, had probably been playing matchmaker, trying to reunite her and her family. "Really?"

"Honestly, Ellie. He told me he was going to the Caribbean for some R and R. All on my own, I thought up the plan to have your assistant toy with your poll results."

"I can see why you'd want to take full credit," Ellie said sarcastically.

"Don't get smart with me," Daddy Eddie warned, then he heaved a sigh. "Look, Ellie, I know you're sleeping with Robby—"

She gasped. "Who told you that?"

"I have eyes," Daddy Eddie assured her. "It might have had something to do with all your improper behavior near the water cooler, and on the desk, and in the kitchen, and near the copier, and—"

Ellie had straightened her shoulders, sitting up straight. "I get your drift, Daddy."

"While doing business with the accounting firm," he confessed, "I got the idea that Percy Anders might not be the sharpest knife in the drawer, and I just thought that maybe if you went out with him and compared him to Robby that whatever your differences, you two would…"

"You," she said simply.

"I was playing matchmaker. I admit it."

"And you told Angelina that's what you were doing, too. Except she thought Percy was somebody from my past. Why, you sly old man."

"I miss you, Ellie," he said matter-of-factly. "Why don't you just come home? Robby misses you, too. I don't know what happened up there, but isn't it something you could talk to me or Mama about? Maybe we can help."

A visceral wave of sensation hit Ellie. She knew what had happened. She and Robby couldn't keep their hands off each other. Even now, she could feel them slowly traveling over her body. A shudder shook her shoulders. Still, she couldn't tell her father all that.

"He's been moping around here since the day you left!" her father exclaimed. "And if something doesn't happen soon I'm going to lose my business because of it. He's like a lost pup without you, Ellie."

"Robby Robriquet…a lost pup?" She couldn't help but laugh. "I doubt that."

"It's true, Ellie. And I'm not happy, either. Now, I'm going to get off the phone, and let you think all this over. In exactly fifteen minutes—let's synchronize our watches—I'm going to call you back and hear your answer. I think you should sign whatever deal Robby brought there. Then come home so Mama and me can see you every day. I want to drive you crazy, as I always have. You can marry Robby, have a grand time, give me plenty of grandbabies, and then we'll all live happily ever after."

Having finished that speech, her father promptly hung up.

She couldn't help but smile. Her father really was a crazy old coot. No doubt, he would call her back in fifteen minutes, just as he'd said. He didn't seem to be lying about Robby putting together the deal, and Daddy Eddie had probably been the only one involved in setting her up with Percy. That particular piece of deviousness had her father written all over it.

Her throat squeezed tightly, and for a few minutes, she just sat there thinking. She felt breathless and strangely jittery inside. Robby had come here, hat in hand, but he hadn't been able to admit it. That changed everything. She'd been so sure he'd come at her father's bidding, but he wanted her back. She wanted him, too. And if the truth be told, she'd trade the city for Banner any day. New York had been kind to her, but it didn't represent the life she truly wanted.

She wanted to go home, plain and simple. Glancing down, she frowned, staring into the open drawer of the desk. Her feet touched the floor and she sat up to lift out an open folder. "Four-four-five-eight-nine-one-one-four-five-two," she whispered.

That had been the number attached to her real dream man. She turned on her computer and searched her archived files, until she found the one that linked numbers and names. Not that she cared. Robby was the only man for her. Just as she thought that, she found the number once more and she ran her finger across a column on the screen and gasped. "Robby Robriquet?"

He was her real dream man? The man her poll had weeded out from among so many? "I'm good at what I do," she whispered.

Slipping her feet into her shoes, she rose, crossed the room, lifted Robby's duffel and hoisted it onto her shoulder. Taking a deep breath, she scanned the room, but realized she needed to take absolutely nothing else. With a phone call, she secured a flight she could make if she hurried. That was the one good thing about such a big city, she thought. It had the biggest airports, too, and that meant she could leave as soon as possible.

As she reached the door and crossed the threshold, the phone rang. "Daddy Eddie," she murmured, a malicious glint coming into her eyes as she stared at the receiver. Letting the phone ring, she switched off the lights, then shut the door and locked it. Let Daddy Eddie wonder, she thought.

And then she stepped into the early night.

13

ROBBY STRODE THROUGH the airport concourse toward the outer doors. Unencumbered by bags, he should have felt lighter, but instead, he'd touched down in Banner with a heavy heart. It felt heavier still when he saw Sheriff Kemp, wearing a tan uniform, lounging against a wall. He was a massive man with shaggy blond hair and brown eyes. When he saw Robby, he came toward him saying, "I need to talk to you, Robby."

Robby groaned. It had been a long twenty-four hours. He hadn't even kissed Ellie goodbye. He'd been too mad. But on the plane, the truth sank in. Maybe he'd never see her again. Now, to add insult to injury, it looked as if he'd have to handle some fiasco involving his father. Maybe he'd been involved in the troubles in New York, after all.

"At least let me get home and shower before I have to sort out my old man again," he muttered.

"I've been trying to call your cell, but you never answered."

He'd left the phone in his duffel at Ellie's. So there was something else he'd never see again. The papers for the deal were in his bag, too. "I don't want to talk about Charlie right now. Officer Hoffman said he called you, since I told him my dad might be mixed up in what was happening to Ellie. Then I guess you called him back with information. I figure Charlie got mixed up with Max Sweeney again, and as it turns out, Max knows an unsavory character in New York named Big

Frank, who caused Ellie some trouble. Anyway, the last I saw of Big Frank and his two nasty sidekicks, they were on their way to jail."

"So is Max."

"It's about time," Robby said, not particularly caring about the specific charges. Although he didn't want to ask, he did. "And Charlie?"

"There's something I need to tell you about your father," the sheriff began.

Just as he started to protest, Robby saw his father near the front door and exploded. "What's he doing here?" Robby's chest squeezed painfully with emotions he couldn't begin to define. Not now, he thought. Not when he'd just left Ellie. "This is the wrong time for me to run into him," he muttered.

"I wanted to prepare you."

Never mind. Charlie had sensed his son's attention and was starting to walk in his direction. As much as Robby hated to admit it, his father looked like a new man. He was tan and fit. Neatly dressed, too, wearing pressed slacks and a V-neck pullover sweater. He looked so much like an older version of Robby that Robby had often wondered just what, if anything, his mother had contributed to his DNA.

Years ago, long after she'd died, he'd stared at pictures, comparing his features to hers, but he was his father's child, if only in looks, never in morals. Robby's gaze drifted over the older man, the cragginess of his facial features, the still full head of dark, curling hair.

Against his will, Robby felt his heart tug, and he braced himself for all the things he knew better than to feel—care, concern, compassion and the like. They were weak emotions, merely love for the father who never was, the man who was supposed to feed him, clothe him and play ball with him. The other man, his real father, not the fantasy father, had run over Shirley Fey because he was drunk.

One wouldn't know it now, though. Charlie's nearly identical blue eyes searched Robby's face. "Did he tell you?"

"Tell me what!" Robby exploded. "What have you done this time? Dammit, I just got off a plane! I've been to New York and back in a day!"

And once more, his relationship with Ellie was over. She'd never trust him. In a way, he didn't blame her. Standing on the street, outside the mobsters' social club, he'd found himself admitting the truth, if only to himself. Maybe he had manipulated Daddy Eddie. When he was offered the job, he could have declined. Or insisted it be shared, and that Ellie never know her own father had favored him. He'd angled for the position all along, hadn't he?

And why? Because he never wanted to be like his father. He wanted to support a family, instead. He wanted to pamper Ellie, and give her everything he'd never had. He wanted a traditional home because he'd never known one. Now he'd lost her. And as usual, it was connected to the screwed-up father-son relationship foisted upon him by this man.

"I didn't get a chance to tell him," Sheriff Kemp was saying to Charlie.

"You just got out of jail," Robby said, trying to control his temper. "How could you mess something up so soon? Was it gambling? Do you have a debt? Do you need money?"

At least Robby could help in that regard now. As a kid, he'd always felt helpless when Charlie had financial problems. Nobody else said anything, so Robby demanded, "What's going on?"

"I hoped the officer in New York would break the news to you," Charlie began. "I wish there was some way you would never know, but it's bound to come out in court."

"Court? There's already legal trouble?"

"Your dad isn't guilty of Shirley Fey's death," the sheriff interjected. "He did the jail time to—"

"That's all he needs to know," Charlie said flatly, with more authority than Robby had ever heard in his father's voice.

"It's not all he needs to know," Sheriff Kemp returned adamantly, sounding furious. "I'm not going to let you do this, Charlie, not this time."

"Do what?" asked Robby. "And what did you mean when you said he didn't kill Shirley Fey?"

"Johnny Sweeney ran over her with one of his sports cars," the sheriff said. "They had a date. She was taken with him, impressed by his looks and money, the way so many girls have been. They were drinking, partying, and he either came on to her and she didn't want him to, or they fought. Anyway, she got out of the moving car, and at some point he ran over her."

"What are you talking about?" Robby asked in shock.

"Max Sweeney confessed as much," Sheriff Kemp said.

Confused, Robby couldn't even look at Charlie. What the hell was going on here? "Why would Max say that?"

"Because I was persuasive," Sheriff Kemp stated. "He doted on that boy of his, spoiled him rotten, but he was bad news. He had Charlie under his thumb due to his gambling debts, so when Johnny ran over Shirley, Max decided to frame Charlie. He did, too, at least at first. But there were discrepancies in the case…"

Robby stared at his father. "You did eight years because some low-life bookie said he'd forgive your gambling debts?" Why hadn't his father just gotten a job and paid them like a normal person? Damn, if the man wasn't even weaker than he'd thought. His father would do anything to escape a hard day's work.

"That's not why your dad did it," Sheriff Kemp said.

"We've said enough," Charlie said firmly.

"What?" Robby demanded.

"Don't tell him anything more," Charlie warned.

"It'll come out and, besides, he'll hear it all over town. You can't protect him forever."

"Protect me from what!"

"Knowing your dad did the time because Max Sweeney threatened to kill you if he didn't. Max visited your father in jail a lot more than you did, in order to remind him of the death threat against your life."

"Enough," Charlie said once more.

Robby could only stare. His whole world had just slid off-kilter. Everything was topsy-turvy. What was good was bad, and what was bad was good. If it was true, he could never live down the disservice he'd done to his old man. An eight-year sacrifice to save Robby's life would sure wipe the slate clean. At least if his father could ever forgive him.

"I know I wasn't much of a dad," Charlie was saying. "And I was confused for a lot of years. I missed your mother more than life. I loved her more than a man should ever love a woman. I want you to know that. When she passed, I couldn't figure out how to move on, but no apology could ever make up for how you had to fend for yourself and take care of me when you were younger."

Shaken, Robby backed up, found a chair and sat down. Charlie sat beside him. "I didn't want you to feel bad about this," he said. "I didn't want you to know. Now that you do, you have to understand that doing time was good for me. I may not have killed Shirley Fey, but my whole life was a crime. That's how I feel about it now. I had plenty of time for thinking and clean living, and I came out a changed man. It cost eight years, but you were kept safe and I got my own life back.

"I couldn't have kept living the way we used to," he continued, "and I'm sorry I put you through it. That was like a half-life, an endless cycle of pain, but now it's over."

Somehow, Robby ventured a glance at his father. The man had done eight years in jail because a scumbag had threatened his son, and he wasn't even angry. Tears stung Robby's eyes, making them feel gritty. For a moment, he simply put his face into his hands and waited for the emotions to pass. "I'm sorry," he whispered. "I should have known. I should have…"

"Known what?" asked Charlie. "That I was innocent? Why on earth would you have believed that?"

Robby could only shake his head. "Tell me everything that happened," he said hoarsely, his voice a mere whisper. "How did Max approach you? Did he frame you first, then when the case began having problems, force your confession, the way the sheriff just said?" He wanted to hear everything again, but now straight from Charlie's mouth…in the words of his own dad.

"That's exactly right, son," Charlie said, then he went on to tell Robby the whole story again. He was speaking a truth that had been lost and forgotten, just like the love between them, for a very long time.

HOURS LATER, ROBBY was still seated on his couch. He'd sat there so long that he felt almost numb. So much had happened in twenty-four hours that he couldn't process it all. When the doorbell rang, he startled. Frowning, he rose and went to answer it. Maybe it was Charlie? Robby's heart lurched with hope. He'd made plans to have breakfast with his father at Delia's first thing the following morning.

"Imagine that," he murmured. "Family breakfasts with Charlie Robriquet." Maybe his dad had forgotten something he'd wanted to say, so he was stopping by.

Robby shook his head. Had his old man, a guy he'd hated for years, really spent eight years in jail just to protect him?

How many fathers could have made that sacrifice for their son? In minutes, Robby had gone from having the world's worst father to the world's best. Lithely, he caught the door-knob, turned it and swung open the door.

It was the wrong time for another shock. Robby's heart broke when he saw her. "Ellie."

Framed in the doorway, she was wearing the same clothes as she had in New York. Her hair was more windblown, the raincoat and brown suit more rumpled, as if she'd slept in the outfit on the plane. He watched as she ran a thumb under the strap to his duffel, lifting it off her shoulder. She held it out by the strap. "You left this at my place."

He couldn't help but smile. She'd said the words as if she'd walked across the street, instead of traveled across a few states. "Thanks for bringing it over," he said just as casually.

She squinted. "Are you okay?"

"Sure."

"You look a little…"

Pale? Shaken? "I know. I got some real strange news about Charlie."

"I heard."

He raised an eyebrow. "You did?"

"Sheriff Kemp and Officer Hoffman were calling back and forth, Sheriff Kemp because Charlie called him, and Officer Hoffman because we called him. Officer Hoffman told me."

"That's Banner, Mississippi, for you. Gossip travels fast along this grapevine." His eyes were roving over every inch of the woman he'd been so sure he'd never see again. "I'm glad you're here," he said simply. His fingers itching to touch her, he set aside the duffel and snuggled his hands inside her open coat, settling them on her waist. "Come in."

"I can only stay a while," she said as he pulled her inside and into an embrace, shutting the door with his foot.

She was soft and warm and smelled of roses. The next thing he knew, his cheek was against her cheek, so he could press whispers into her hair. He nuzzled gently, loving the feel of his eyelashes sweeping her skin, and how their bellies suddenly touched, setting off fireworks. "How long exactly?" he murmured.

"How about a lifetime?"

Leaning back a fraction so he could look at her face, he smiled. "That would certainly be long enough to take you to bed, Ellie Lee, which is what I most want to do." Becoming serious, he said, "A lifetime, huh? Just like that?"

She nodded. "Yeah. The day I left for New York, when you were trying to tell me about your promotion, I thought you were going to tell me…"

His heart squeezed tightly as he had a sudden insight. "That I wanted to get married?"

She nodded.

"Well, I do, Ellie."

"You do?"

He nodded. But did she? "What about your company?"

"Since the papers are in your duffel, I read them more carefully on the plane."

His mind was reeling, and the smile on his face was broadening. He'd gotten his dream father and now Ellie had just walked back into his life. "You snoop," he teased.

"I saw your girly magazines, too."

"There were no girly magazines in my duffel bag, Ellie."

"Must have belonged to some other guy then. Anyway, the Lee Polls and Future Trends merger looks like a sweet deal."

"Not as sweet as you."

"Flatterer."

Below the belt, he felt a stir of undeniable, unquenchable

longing. Blood engorged him as he drew her closer, so their hips locked where he was getting hard for her. "We could have kids and I'll be the stay-at-home daddy," he told her.

She shrugged, then slipped her arms more tightly around him, then let her hands slide downward to caress his buttocks, stroking him through his slacks with her fingernails, making him want to moan out loud.

She shook her head. "You're too good at your job to stay home all day, Robby."

"Not without you around the office to keep me on my toes. Besides, I don't care about work anymore."

"Now that's a lie."

"No, Ellie, it's true," he assured her.

"You'd give it all up for me?"

He nodded.

"You know what?" Before he could answer, she said, "I'd give work up for you, too. And somehow, I think Derrick Mills is going to find a good story in all this that will work just fine for his newspaper."

Robby was imagining so many things now, including simply bringing their family to work. The solutions had always been so simple, but he and Ellie hadn't been ready for more, not really.

"I talked to Charlie for a good long while," Robby said, "and it brought home what I had already admitted to myself, Ellie. I did angle for your job, I think. And I know you sensed that. I didn't do it consciously, but I wanted you to have the easy life. I wanted to pamper you and put you on a pedestal. I had it rough, so I've been trying to work as hard as I can, just to make sure I'm worthy of you and your family."

"Sounds like you have a great family of origin yourself."

"I do," he said with emotion. "Can you believe my dad went to jail just to protect me?"

"I think you're like your dad," she whispered. "Same ethical fiber."

When he glanced down, he could see her eyes had turned shiny with unshed tears. Leaning in, he brushed a soft kiss across her lips. "You look gorgeous, lady."

She offered a half smile. "I think we can do so much together. We can hang out with J.D. and Susannah, just like in the good old days."

"Remember the time," he agreed, lightly lifting the engraved charm she wore.

"We both love how we contribute to the world through our work," she rushed on, "and we love Banner, Mississippi, and all our friends."

"We love something else," he whispered.

"What?"

Before his mouth descended to claim a more penetrating kiss, he murmured, "Each other, Ellie."

"Can you prove it?"

Smiling against her lips, he pushed her coat from her shoulders, then unbuttoned the white blouse she wore. Her hands got just as busy, fiddling with his belt and zipper. When her chest was bare and the bra open, he filled his gaze, experiencing a thrill of possession that rocked his very soul. He wasn't wearing shoes, and as she kicked off hers, he unzipped her skirt and let it fall to the floor. Reaching, he grabbed her hand and began walking.

"Where are you taking me?" she asked, the catch in her voice that made clear she damn well knew their destination.

"The bedroom. Surely, you remember where it is."

"It's wherever we make love," she said as they entered the room in which they'd broken up so many months before. He watched as he got on the bed, stripping off her underclothes. He was hard now. With Ellie, it didn't take much to get him aroused. Just a glance, a touch. Seeing her fully naked pushed him over the edge. When he was nude, too, he climbed into bed and ran a palm from her hip to her calves, then caressed her breasts. As he massaged, he kissed her, now using his tongue.

Everything they'd experienced during the taxing day receded into the background. Tomorrow would bring more answers. No doubt, Max and Johnny Sweeney would both do jail time. More of the story would surface. Derrick Mills would write the story, and the merger of Lee Polls and Future Trends would be announced. But those things didn't matter now.

"We do love each other, don't we?" she whispered, her voice holding a touch of awe.

Smiling down as he rolled on top of her, he said softly, "We'll love each other even more in just a minute."

"I'm game."

Sucking in a quick breath, he entered her and caught her scent, his nostrils flaring. Thrusting deep, he felt her catch the rhythm, and soon they were climbing, as they always would together…higher and higher.

He felt her slide her fingers into his hair, and so he tilted his head back slightly to stare deeply into her eyes. He could only sigh as his hips flexed, and he felt her quicken, moving toward her orgasm. She was hot and moaning now. Her creamy, silken thighs were opened wide, and she was bringing him all the way into her body, shuddering.

"I have something else to tell you," she suddenly whispered, her voice ragged. "I forgot."

"What?" he murmured, dropping kisses over her face and lips and neck.

As she arched to meet his slow thrust, her voice strained with passion. "I saw the real polling results…the ones Angelina hid."

"Did you?" Grasping her hands, he urged her arms above her head, so she was fully exposed. Her breasts heaved, the nipples pert as she arched again to take even more of him. As her legs circled around his back, he pleasured her with a deep, bold, burning stroke. "Let me guess," he whispered. "Your original results said I'm your dream man."

She stilled. "How did you know?"

Right before his lips claimed hers for another soul-searing kiss, he nuzzled her hair and feather-kissed her shoulders, and said, "Because, honey, it was me, not your daddy, who tampered with those poll results. I just wanted to make sure you got it right."

She reacted by batting at him. Laughing, he fought back, his whole body tingling and alive with raw sensuality as he grabbed her and hugged her close. Her skin was warm and moist from their love play, and now her nipples brushed his chest, feeling taut. "Just kidding," he quipped, his heart racing as he pushed inside her…stretching her…loving her.

She wound her arms around him and held him so tightly that no breath could pass between them. Then her hands roved over his back, silently urging him to thrust even harder. She could barely catch her breath. "Liar," she accused.

"Guilty," he admitted, panting. "Your results are the real deal."

"We're the real deal," she corrected.

Against her mouth, he huskily asked, "Do you feel ready to sign on the dotted line and seal the agreement?"

"Only if you feel ready to deliver," she challenged. "You know, you're the only one who can, as far as I'm concerned."

"Why only me?" As he held her and began to show her hot loving that would surpass everything they'd ever shared before, she whispered, "Because numbers never lie, Robby. You're my one and only dream man."

* * * * *

*Celebrate 60 years of pure
reading pleasure with Harlequin®!*

*Step back in time and enjoy a
sneak preview of an exciting anthology
from Harlequin® Historical with*
THE DIAMONDS OF WELBOURNE MANOR.

This compelling anthology features three stories about
the outrageous Fitzmanning sisters. Meet Annalise, who
is never at a loss for words… But that can change with
an unexpected encounter in the forest.

*Available May 2009
from Harlequin® Historical.*

"I'm the illegitimate daughter of notoriously scandalous parents, Mr. Milford. Candidates for my hand are unlikely to be lining up at the gates."

"Don't be so quick to discount your charms, my dear. Or the charm of your substantial dowry. Or even your brothers' influence. There are as many reasons to marry as there are marriages."

Annalise snorted. "Oh, yes. Perhaps I shall marry for dynastic reasons, or perhaps for property or influence. After all, a loveless, practical marriage worked out so well for my mother."

"Well, you've routed me on that one. I can think of no suitable rejoinder." Ned rose to his feet and extended his hand. "And since that is the case, let me be the first to wish you a long and happy spinsterhood."

Her mouth gaped open. And then she laughed.

And he froze.

This was the first time, Ned realized. The first time he'd seen her eyes light up and her mouth curl. The first time he'd witnessed her features melded together in glorious accord to produce exquisite beauty.

Unbelievable what a change came over her face. Unheard of what effect her throaty, rasping laughter had on his body. It pounded a beat upon his ear, quickly taken up by his pulse. It echoed through him, finally residing in his stirring nether regions.

So easily she did it, awakened these sensations within him—without any apparent effort at all. And she had called him potentially dangerous? Clearly the intelligent thing for him to do would be to steer clear, to leave her to the tender ministrations of Lord Peter Blackthorne.

"You were right." She smiled up at him as she took his hand and climbed to her feet. "I do feel better."

Ah, well. When had he ever chosen the intelligent path?

He did not relinquish her hand. He used it to pull her in, close enough that he could feel the warmth of her. "At the risk of repeating Lord Peter's mistake and anticipating too much— may I ask if you'll be my partner in battledore tomorrow?"

Her smiled dimmed. Her breath came a little faster. His own had gone shallow, as if he'd just run a race—and lost. He ran his gaze over the appealing lift of her brow and the curious angle of her chin. His index finger twitched.

"I should like that," she said.

His finger trembled again and he lifted it, traced the pink and tender shell of her ear, the unique sweep of her jaw. Her pulse leaped beneath her skin, triggering his own. Slowly he tilted her chin up, waiting for her to object, to step back, to slap his hand away.

She did none of those eminently sensible things. Which left him free to do the entirely impractical thing.

Baby soft, the skin of her lips. Her whole body trembled when he touched her there.

He leaned in. Her eyes closed, even as she stood straight against him, strung as tight as a bow. He pressed his mouth to hers. It was a soft kiss, sweet and chaste. And yet he was hot and hard and as ready as he'd ever been in his life.

She drew back a little. Sighed. Their breath mingled a moment before she slowly backed away.

"Oh," she breathed. Her dark eyes were full of wonder and something that looked like fear. He took a step toward her, but she only shook her head. His outstretched hand fell to his side as she turned to disappear into the wood. This was the first time, Ned realized. The first time, since he'd come to the house party at Welbourne Manor, that he'd seen her eyes light up.

* * * * *

Follow Ned and Annalise's
story in May 2009 in
THE DIAMONDS OF WELBOURNE MANOR.
Available May 2009
from Harlequin® Historical.

Available in the series romance section,
or in the historical romance section,
wherever books are sold.

We'll be spotlighting a different series
every month throughout 2009
to celebrate our 60th anniversary.

Look for Harlequin® Historical in May!

Celebrations begin with
a sumptuous Regency house party!

Join three scandalous sisters in

THE DIAMONDS OF
WELBOURNE MANOR

Glittering, scintillating, sensual fun
by Diane Gaston, Deb Marlowe
and Amanda McCabe.

**60 years of Harlequin,
600 years of romance
in Harlequin Historical!**

You're invited to join our Tell Harlequin Reader Panel!

By joining our new reader panel you will:

- Receive Harlequin® books—they are FREE and yours to keep with no obligation to purchase anything!
- Participate in fun online surveys
- Exchange opinions and ideas with women just like you
- Have a say in our new book ideas and help us publish the best in women's fiction

In addition, you will have a chance to win great prizes and receive special gifts! See Web site for details. Some conditions apply. Space is limited.

To join, visit us at
www.TellHarlequin.com.

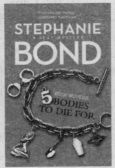
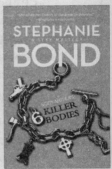

REQUEST YOUR FREE BOOKS!

2 FREE NOVELS
PLUS 2
FREE GIFTS!

HARLEQUIN®

Blaze™

Red-hot reads!

HB09R

Harlequin® Historical
Historical Romantic Adventure!

If you enjoyed reading
Joanne Rock in the
Harlequin® Blaze™ series,
look for her new book
from Harlequin® Historical!

THE KNIGHT'S RETURN
Joanne Rock

Missing more than his memory,
Hugh de Montagne sets out to find his
true identity. When he lands in a small
Irish kingdom and finds a new liege in the
Irish king, his hands are full with his new
assignment: guarding the king's beautiful,
exiled daughter. Sorcha has had her heart
broken by a knight in the past. Will she be
able to open her heart to love again?

Available April
wherever books are sold.

COMING NEXT MONTH

Available April 28, 2009

#465 HOT-WIRED Jennifer LaBrecque
From 0–60
Drag racer/construction company owner Beau Stillwell has his hands full trying to mess up his sister's upcoming wedding. The guy just isn't good enough for her. But when Beau meets Natalie Bridges, the very determined wedding planner, he realizes he needs to change gears and do something drastic. Like drive sexy, uptight Natalie absolutely wild...

#466 LET IT RIDE Jillian Burns
What better place for grounded flyboy Cole Jackson to blow off some sexual steam than Vegas, baby! Will his campaign to seduce casino beauty Jordan Brenner crash and burn, once she discovers what he really wants to bet?

#467 ONCE A REBEL Debbi Rawlins
Stolen from Time, Bk. 3
Maggie Dawson is stunned when the handsomest male *ever* appears from the future, insisting on her help! Cord Braddock's out of step in the 1870s Wild West, although courting sweet, sexy Maggie comes as naturally to him as the sun rising over the Dakota hills....

#468 GOING DOWN HARD Tawny Weber
When Sierra Donovan starts receiving indecent pictures of herself—with threats attached—she knows she's going to need help. But the last person she needs it from is sexy security expert Reece Carter. Although, if Sierra's back has to be against the wall, she can't think of anyone she'd rather put her there....

#469 AFTERBURN Kira Sinclair
Uniformly Hot!
Air force captain Chase Carden knows life will be different now that he's back from Iraq—he's already been told he'll be leading the Thunderbird Squadron. Little does he guess that his biggest change will come in the person of Rina McAllister, his last one-night stand...who's now claiming to be his wife!

#470 MY SEXY GREEK SUMMER Marie Donovan
A wicked vacation is what Cara Sokol has promised herself, although she has to keep her identity a secret! Hottie Yannis Petridis is exactly what she's looking for *and* he's good with secrets—he's got one of his own!

HBCNMBPA0409